'Til
Niagara Falls

Katerie Morin

Po84 Productions
Cambridge, Massachusetts

Katerie Morin/Po84 Productions
Harvard Square/PO Box 380084
Cambridge, Massachusetts/02238
www.po84poductions.com

Publisher's Note: This is a work of fiction. Names, characters, places and incidents are either the product of the author's imagination or are used fictitiously.

Book Layout ©2013 BookDesignTemplates.com

Ordering Information:
Quantity sales. Special discounts are available on quantity purchases by corporations, associations, and others. For details, contact the "Special Sales Department" at the address above.

'Til Niagara Falls/ Katerie Morin. -- 1st ed.
ISBN 978-1-948133-01-2

To my parents,
Paul and Ann Louise,
who took me to the Falls
and asked me why she did it.

"But look! here come more crowds, pacing straight for the water, and seemingly bound for a dive. Strange! Nothing will content them but the extremest limit of the land… They must get just as nigh the water as they possibly can without falling in."

—Moby Dick

The Robbery – Annie

When the other passengers have drifted off in that half-sleep that comes to those sitting upright, I take my place in the aisle. I stand facing the direction of the engine and let the sensation of the train's speed take me.

At first, all I feel is the rumble beneath my feet and the sway of the car on the rails. I close my eyes and wait, lifting my hand from the back of the bench so that I stand with arms raised like a diver. Then I feel it, the pull forward, as if I were a fish at the end of a line being flung towards the shore.

I came overland by stagecoach, which felt like being carried in a giant's boot as he staggered west. Going back, our speed is breathtaking. I wonder how fast we're going— twenty, maybe even thirty miles an hour?

The car's windows are closed tight against the billowing ash of the engine, and the air is stale and humid from the sleepers, but standing alone in the train's aisle I am a comet streaking through the sky.

"Are you all right, Ma'am?"

I open my eyes to find myself face to face with a porter. In the half dark his round spectacles are like pennies over his eyelids. I shiver at the image and stumble sideways towards my seat.

"Thank you, a touch of rheumatism, that is all," I say as I maneuver back into my place on the hard bench. The gray that has begun to streak my hair allows me certain eccentricities and after a moment, he keeps going down the aisle.

Third class is the first passenger car behind the express, closest to the engine and its choking clouds of ash. I'm sure the porter is heading towards first class, at the far rear of the train, where the walls are lined with gleaming walnut and the individual sleeping compartments are separated by heavy crimson drapes. I'm sure in first class the windows are open to the night and the passengers dream of flying.

Across from me a little boy lies asleep with his head in his mother's lap. His face is slack with trust, the sandy fringe of his hair falling across his cheek. I frown at the pretty picture the two of them make. I will not let myself remember what that feels like, that warm weight of peace. I turn my face towards the dark mirror of the window and press my forehead against the cool glass. At least the woman's husband is still asleep.

The three of them boarded at one of the whistle stop towns that exist to supply the train with water and wood, a tiny dot on the map, just west of the Utah line. I remember a rickety depot, a tank house and a woodshed. Nothing else that even hinted that people lived anywhere amidst the scrub brush that unfolded in four directions.

"Why does the train say that?" the boy had asked his mother when the train whistle blasted.

"It's just a whistle," she said "It doesn't mean anything."

"It's the sound the steam makes when the train engineer opens the exhaust valve," I told him. "The engineer has to keep the steam's pressure high enough to make the train go, but not so high that the boiler explodes." I couldn't stop myself, years in front of the classroom had made it impossible for me to ignore the little boy's question.

"Steam's just water gone crazy from the heat," the mother told the boy in a tone that meant, "don't listen to her, she's as crazy as the steam." It was then she noticed her husband noticing me and narrowed her eyes in my direction. I guess my hair isn't gray enough for her, she saw me as a threat. I think she misunderstood his interest. The look he gave me, it was the one he might give a horse that can count.

I wonder how long it will take before I stop answering the questions of children. For years I've seen the world as a collection of natural laws to be explained and understood, when will that fade? How long till I can resist the urge to save empty tin cans in the hopes of making Bunsen burners from them? My eyes have been on the ground, looking for the glint of nails or copper wire scraps. I need to raise my head, not everything needs to be saved till it finds a purpose.

The train whistle wakes me. Outside the window the landscape is a flat expanse of brown with sage that's only barely green. I hear a pop, then a series of rapid pops, like water dancing on a well-oiled skillet. The train bucks beneath me and I fall into the aisle.

The world seems to collapse on top of me in an avalanche of boxes and bags. We shudder to a stop. Around me I hear groans. My legs are buried under luggage fallen from the upper rack. I kick my feet, and while the bags slide, I'm still stuck. When I lift my head a porter is running down the aisle towards me. I raise my hand for help but he steps over the pile that pins me down and keeps going.

"One moment, my dear!" someone says and I feel the bags on my legs slide down and over my heels. I pick up my head and an older gentleman in pinstripes holds out his hand, wheezing slightly. I take it and struggle to standing. Now I can see why the porter left me in the aisle.

Outside there is a man on horseback, his face concealed by a black bandana, his rifle leveled at the windows of the passenger car. There are so many passengers looking through the glass at him that I briefly wonder whether the car will tip over from all that weight on one side. The popping noises must have been gun shots aimed at the train's engineer. We are being robbed.

"Do you think we've been stopped by the James gang?" the mother asks her husband, her hands covering the boy's ears. "I heard that with each hold up they leave a letter stating how they want the robbery to appear in the paper, how they want their names printed, how they pulled it off. They just leave blanks for the amount of cash taken."

"Saves reporters some work," her husband says.

"The James Gang doesn't operate outside Wyoming, we're three hundred miles from the border," my savior points out, wiping his face with a white handkerchief. "Now, there should be six of them, I'm sure of it," he went on, "2-2-2 that's the pattern. Two for the engineer, two for the express car, and two to watch over us, to make sure we don't do anything daring."

"I didn't read none of that 2-2-2 nonsense in the paper," the husband says. "And I keep up on all the railway news."

"I'm afraid that's not from the paper. Last spring I saw 'The Collis Train Robbery' at the National Theater in San Francisco. I was lucky enough to see Chris Evans's own wife and daughter play themselves in the production." From the way he said it, you'd think he'd seen Charles Dickens perform *A Christmas Carol,* instead of the kin of a convicted railway bandit in the story of his prison escape.

"Evans was driven to it by the railroad's stealing his land," calls someone closer to the door, "They got what they deserved!"

"Like hell!" comes another opinion.

"Some claimed the play was lurid, but I found it very informative," the older gentleman continues. "Whoever these men are, they're clearly gentlemen."

"Why do you say that?" I ask. "They seem the farthest thing from gentlemen to me."

"He only means we're not dead, they didn't wreck the tracks to stop us," a man at my elbow says.

Destroying the rails to cause a train to crash had been the pattern for train robberies five years ago. Back then bandits would first loot the express car, then rifle through the bodies of the deceased for whatever they had in their pockets.

"Look, they've got the safe!" someone calls.

A mule comes into view, dragging a green Wells Fargo safe by a length of rope. I curse myself for a fool, we must be carrying silver from the Magdalena mines. New Mexico is riddled with dark holes of the stuff, not enough to cause a silver rush, but enough to draw some families clear across the continent. There was enough to draw me.

Finally, they have the safe on the ground. They dump the Pinkerton guard next to it. Then one of the robbers starts going horse to horse, throwing open every saddlebag.

There's shouting, cursing. The man on horseback outside our window turns towards the confusion.

"Nate forgot the goddamn dynamite!"

One of the bandits is shoved forward. No dynamite means no way to open the safe. They've stopped the train for nothing. How long will it take the engineer to get the engines working again? The bandit, Nate, points to the passenger cars. I shrink back from the window.

"Get 'em out here!" one of the bandits yells.

"What can they mean?" the mother asks her husband.

"They're going to rob us," the older gentleman says and in seconds there's a scramble away from the windows. People start emptying their pockets, fumbling with bags and underneath cushions—they're hiding their money.

I hear a click and turn. There's a bandit in the doorway of the car, his pistol leveled. Everyone freezes and the bandit gestures for us to exit the car. Slowly, we file out, the armed man behind us.

We stand in the shadow of the train. My heels crunch in the gravel that lines the tracks. The shadow is barely a foot deep. If the train had been robbed an hour earlier there would be no shade, we'd be standing in full desert sun.

I can see six bandits, so perhaps the play was right with its 2-2-2. The horseman keeps his rifle leveled at us while Nate walks down the line, a gunnysack held open in front of each passenger. They empty their pockets, but he isn't satisfied, he takes watches and necklaces. I watch as everything the passengers couldn't hide falls into the bag. I clasp my hands together, put them over my heart, press down on the outline of my wedding ring where it lies sewn to the strap of my bodice. Nate stands in front of me and I can't move.

He grabs my reticule and dumps it over his bag. My papers, my photographs, an advertisement for a typewriter from E. Remington and Sons, they all flutter to the ground. He shakes it again, my salve falls and rolls into the dust.

"Where's your money?" he asks me. His eyes are wild. He forgot the dynamite. The mistake may have cost him his life, I won't let it cost me mine.

"I don't have any," I tell him, but I'm too loud. I try to hold his gaze and slowly lower my hands to my sides, let them hang loose just over the roll of bills sewn into my petticoat.

"For heaven's sake," the woman next to me says, "Just give it to him." She reaches past me to drop her wedding ring into the bag. I noticed she removed it when Nate was still several passengers away, she was too quick, too happy, to do so.

"I don't have any," I repeat when the truth is I have everything I own sewn to my underskirt. Each bill took a year of scrimping to put something by, a year of scraping against blackboards from St. Louis to San Antonio and finally, New Mexico. Each bill earned in a place hotter and drier and more desperate then the last.

The bandit picks up my ticket, I watch his lips move as he reads my destination.

"No one travels from New Mexico to Michigan without a dime," he says finally.

"They do if they teach school," I say.

There's a barking laugh and although his face is masked, the horseman's eyes and voice tell me he's leering at me.

"School m'arms and spinsters always hide their money in their petticoats," he says.

The bandit in front of me grabs my left hand and holds it up. There's no ring.

"Lift your skirt and give me your money," Nate says.

"I will not lift my skirt," I'm loud again. I can't help it. I give him "The Look." It has stopped boys with spitballs but it doesn't stop him. He draws his gun.

"Lift your skirt," he repeats.

I can't move. He presses the barrel of his gun to the side of my head. The metal is cool, the leather of the holster has kept it insulated from the heat of the day. If I wait, the metal will warm from the contact with my skin. It will conduct back up the barrel to his hand.

But no, that must be what the ivory handle is for, to save his hand from the heat of the bullet firing, each one, a small explosion making the metal hot enough to scorch.

"Well?" The question is a growl in my ear. It is the sound of a dog getting ready to pounce.

He is going to kill me. I try to push the thought away, to think of a way out. But it persists, he is going to kill me. And once I am dead, will he roll me over? Lift my skirt over my head? Rifle through my petticoats in front of the boy and his mother?

I want to scream "No! No! No!" It's the thinking of a child—the knife is shiny but it's sharp, the fire is bright but it burns. I want it to be different. It will be different.

"No." The word escapes before I can swallow it.

"Goddamn it! Lift your skirt or I'll blow your brains out!" he snarls. But take my money and you take my life, it's the same thing.

"I'd rather be without brains than honor," I reply. Let them think it is shame that keeps me from obeying. I close my eyes and in a second my lashes are wet. I hear a soft crunch of gravel as a couple of passengers shift their weight. Please, let my words give a kick to their backbones. Please, let someone rescue me. Please, let him falter. Let him put the gun away.

I hear Nate drop the bag. He takes the gun from my head. It will be different. He is putting the gun away.

I open my eyes to a blur of silver, a knife angling towards my skirt. I feel the sting of metal on my thigh and scream. Nate slashes at the calico of my dress. There are shouts from the passengers, but no one moves, no one helps. I slap at him, try to push him back, but in seconds, the front of my dress is cut away.

Another slash and he takes the pocket of fabric I had sewn to my petticoat. He hands it up to the guard who opens it and fans out the bills. I fall to my knees.

"A roll of bills like this is worth killing for," the horseman tells me and then holds them up for the other bandits to see. "Count yourself lucky that I'm in a good mood."

"Please," I say. I'm begging on my knees, my hands clasped together. "I'd rather be without brains than money. Please." He drops the money in the sack and calls them all to mount.

"Please," I say to the dust cloud that rolls towards us from the horses' hooves.

"Please," I say as I pull together the torn edges of my skirt.

The porter offers me his handkerchief. I press it to my leg and watch as a thin line of red soaks through the cotton.

"You're lucky, it isn't deep," he says to me. He lifts me up and carries me back towards the passenger car. Over his shoulder I can see the conductor has assembled the rest of the porters to drag the safe back towards the express car, six of them standing in for the bandits' pack mule.

As they watch that slow parade, the passengers chatter like hens clucking in a yard, happy with relief. They have all escaped with their lives, all except for me.

The porter lowers me into the first seat of the car, then takes off his coat and arranges it over the front of my dress like an apron. The aisle is still cluttered with baggage and he pries loose a suitcase and places it beneath my feet as a footstool.

While he works, I put my left hand behind my back and slide it down into the cushions. I feel around for any money that could have been hidden in the rush before the bandits forced us outside.

My hand closes on a folded piece of paper. I don't look at it, just slide it into my shirt cuff and pray that it's a bill. As the passengers file past me to their seats, I lean forward, wincing and placing both hands over the cut on my leg. The porter asks me if I'd like a cup of water and I shake my head.

"Could you please fetch my bag, I'd like to change into my other dress," I say to him. He puts his fingers to his cap before he leaves because I am a lady. Or at least, I was a lady. Now I am a thief. And I'm as good as dead.

2 The Interview – Annie

From the corner of my eye, I catch a flash of blue flame in the hallway, a ghostly flare the color of copper burning. Before I can move, the landlady races to the door.

"No fire breathing in the house!" she shouts. "And I'd better not find any circus critters in your rooms or you'll be out on your asses!" she slaps her hand against the doorjamb. I can't see the person she's yelling at but from her stance it looks as if she's hectoring a child.

As she turns back to me I see a woman, a dwarf no higher than my waist, in a blue satin gown. The little woman disappears up the stairs, her hand reaching above her to the railing.

"Carnival's in town for a week," the landlady says turning back to me. "I've got the crowd of ladies upon me—bearded, tattooed, dwarved—and a gal who stands there while a man I wouldn't let in my front door throws knives at her, blindfolded."

"Good lord, they're not staying here!" I know it's silly, but I feel my hands tighten on the handle of my carpetbag, as if it could hold me up, keep me from slipping any further down. She shrugs.

"It's like you said, it's only temporary."

That's what I told her when I rang the bell, temporary lodging, a few weeks at the most. I look around the room. It is clean but dingy, as if the walls, like the linen, are yellowing with age. It is only September, but there's a chill in the air. This close to the lake you need a constant fire to battle the damp.

"Is it always so cold?" I ask.

"Fifty cents a week for room and board. Coal is extra. Stove's in the corner," she says, dropping a patchwork quilt on the bed. "You keep it as warm as you can afford." She closes the door. Ten in the morning and already my stomach is rumbling. Dinner is at six, an ocean of time until then.

I sit on the bed and open *The Saginaw News*. The "Help Wanted—Male," spans two pages: pharmacy assistants, secretaries, clerks and laborers. I quickly scan for any teacher listings, they're most often listed here. I can teach anything, but there's nothing. Enrollment is down, that's what I've heard from every principal, every headmaster.

I turn the page to "Help Wanted—Female." The listing is shorter, a half page of wet nurses and housemaids. I circle a few with my oil pencil. The cold in the room makes my hands ache, but it's the thought of all that hot water and lye soap that makes me shiver.

I crumple the page and think about sticking it in the stove. It may yet get colder, so I tuck it into a chink in the wall below the window where I feel a draft. What I need is a position as a governess. I'll even take room and board in lieu of salary. A private position is often not printed in the paper. I need connections.

I reach into my bag and pull out my bankbook. I flip to the last printed page. It still reads twelve dollars, all that's left of the twenty-dollar bill I stole from the cushions of the train.

I upend my reticule over the bed. My diploma falls out and my letters of recommendation. There's an envelope of newspaper clippings about the train robbery with a picture of the men who stole my life. The articles are well creased. I should burn them.

I turn the bag inside out and squeeze the fabric to see if even one coin has found its way into the lining.

Then I hear them, their tread on the stairs and their laughter. The carnival women must be going to work. I'm sure they'll return in the early morning, another parade.

I want to open my door to watch them, but this is how they make their living, showing off their tragedies for money, letting streams of farmers and dockworkers stare at them and laugh. I won't steal a penny from them by looking for free.

I turn the reticule back to right and slip the papers back inside. There is no more delaying it. I must go to the bank. I must steel myself to beg.

Robert has a folder on me, so thick I could call it a dossier. I don't know what it contains. The newspaper clippings I mailed to him, perhaps. I brought my teacher's certificate with me for his review, my letters of recommendation, my proposal for a purchase of three Remington typewriters. Each sheet of paper has been met with the same scowl.

I shift in my seat, my chair is low and his desk is high. I try to remember to be grateful. To be seen here, rather than at the bank, is a favor, Robert's version of *noblesse oblige*. I should appreciate it, or at least do a better job at feigning appreciation. I try to catch his eye, to smile warmly. Instead I feel as if I'm shrinking down through the chair, through the thick rug and the wide planked floor, into the black of the root cellar that I know lies beneath us. I look at the desk.

It was Father's and it gleams from the patient application of linseed oil. That was my job, once.

"Not a penny, not a single dime," Robert says and firmly leans back in his chair. "You haven't proved you can manage money." He pushes my letters back to me as if they're contaminated with something.

"But I paid my last loan back on time, with interest," I hunch forward and try to read my dossier upside down. He snaps it closed.

"You were twenty-three then, look at you now!" he says with disgust. I can't help but put a hand to my hair. He hasn't seen me since it began to turn gray. I haven't seen him since he started to paunch. He's gone jowly.

"I'm younger than you, Robert, remember? I'm your baby sister—" I try to plead, but what comes out is pure rage.

"—You managed to lose your entire pension the week you retired!" he says.

"I was robbed! Everyone on the train was robbed!" I am shaking, "I wrote to you, I sent you the newspaper clippings."

"Father knew this would happen!" he shouts loud enough to scatter the papers in front of him, even the desk seems to quiver.

Father knew this would happen. He says it likes it's a Bible passage, an unquestioned truth to be memorized.

"Father told you nothing good would come of marrying David Taylor," he spits David's name as if it were a bug that had flown into his mouth. "Father said 'if you marry him, you will live in penury!' And now that Father's passed you think you can crawl back here, begging—"

"— Typewriters, Robert! Soon everything will be done on typewriters. It's faster, cleaner, more efficient. The Remington #2, it's the best thing on the market. There's this thing called carbon paper," I should have brought a sample with me.

"You tuck it between two blank pages and when you type, the letters press into both pages. Copies are made with the original, at the same time. The reduction in errors of transcription, it will save real money," I must get him to think of money, not of David, not of me. "According to the newspaper, the Federal government is already using them. But it is a skill that must be learned, that must be practiced. I could open a secretarial school with just three Remington's. They're only $150 a piece—"

"—The robbery on the Santa Fe line was a month ago. What have you been living on since then?" he asks. I recognize his tone from my classroom, it's the taunt of an adolescent boy.

When I had reached my hands down into the cushions of the train, my hand had closed around a twenty-dollar bill. I stare at Robert, my face neutral. I won't confess that the bandits turned me into a thief.

"I sold everything I owned," I tell him.

He reaches across the desk and grabs my left hand. He squeezes my fingers together hard. The metal of my wedding band digs into my skin.

"You haven't seen fit to sell David's ring," he says and flings my hand back at me.

My stomach roils and I nearly wretch. Robert lives in father's house, he sits at father's desk, he swims in father's anger. He will not help me. He will never help me.

"I will not sell David's ring," I tell him and I stand to leave.

"You can't still be in love with him," Robert says. He has gone frothy at the corners of his mouth.

"Why not? You still hate him," I say. And for the second time in my life, I vow never to come back to this house.

Greta is waiting for me in the foyer. There is nothing left of the laughing girl from school. She is shrunk, as if Robert has been feeding off of her. She's tiny now, small enough to hide in his shadow. She hands me my hat and gloves.

"It's a way for him to show how much he loved your father, by hating everything your father hated," Greta says. She says it softly. Perhaps she is never allowed to make a sound.

"If Robert wants to be like Father, he should give me a loan the way Father did when I went to teacher's college," I'm practically shouting. Let Robert hear me, let Robert remember. Father had been cold and calculating. He had made me go to the bank, then refused to meet with me himself. He sent me to a junior loan officer for approval. He made me pay interest.

"Your father loaned you money because he was betting you would fail. He never believed you'd finish school, or get a job teaching. He thought you'd come running home, the repentant prodigal daughter, tethered to this house by an unpayable debt," she says as she helps me pull on my gloves. She can see I'm struggling. My fingers are stiff again.

But I never came home, not even to show Father my diploma. I made my loan payments to the junior officer. I proved my father wrong. I stayed away and I stayed alive.

"I envy you," Greta whispers as she gives me a hug, "you're an independent creature."

"Independence is expensive," I tell her. I feel her tuck something into my waistband. It's a thin envelope.

"It's not much, my grocery money for the week. It will do your brother good to feel a little hungry," she says. She's still whispering. Whatever the amount in the envelope, it will cost her dearly. My eyes water.

"Thank you, thank you," I murmur and hug her again.

"Greta!" Robert shouts from the study. I don't even need to open my arms so she can go to him, she melts like vapor and disappears.

I let myself out onto the porch. The last time I left this house it was down a ladder in the dark, down into David's arms from my bedroom window. Coming home had been a mistake. "Only look forward," David had said so many times.

But I keep looking back, retreating until I'm atop Adrian's Hill. I sit on the ground with my back against David's headstone and let them come, the dogs of grief that have followed me since David's death—no, since our boy, Thomas, died of scarlet fever. I put my hand on the cold ground, above the bodies of my husband and baby. I cry till there are no more tears.

I will have to begin again.

Six o'clock and the meat on my plate is withered and gray. I saw at it with a dull knife. Beside it lies a serving of limp, gray cabbage. I keep sawing. After my interview with Robert I fear I may look back on this meal with longing.

I stayed on Adrian's Hill until the sunset then walked back to the boarding house through the center of town. In the window of the Saginaw Majestic I had seen Robert and Greta eating dinner. Robert had a steak, rare. It ran red into the boiled potatoes on the plate. There was also a mash, it looked like carrots and turnips. If I had stayed, I could have watched him eat a slice of pie or swirl a glass of cognac in his fleshy hands. It was like having a ticket to a theater that only showed cruelty.

I knew he couldn't see me as I watched him. The refraction of the light in the dining room compared to the darkness outside the window rendered me invisible. If he'd looked up, he would have seen his own reflection on the dark surface of the night.

The landlady clears my empty plate and serves dessert, three prunes stewed in a juice that runs brown rings around the plate. If I think, I will wretch. I swallow them without chewing, without tasting. I choke them down. I must begin again.

In bed, the meal lies heavy. I dream of the knife as it slices downward. I am back on the train. I am kneeling in the dust and then—

Laughter!

I wake in the dark and hear the carnival women returning from work, climbing the stairs.

My heart is pounding and I stumble for the door and fling it open. I stare at them, a bearded woman, a young woman covered in tattoos, another wearing a snake around her neck like a woolen scarf. I watch its tongue flicker towards me, tasting the air. The women carry baskets of fruit, loaves of dark bread and bottles of wine. The longer I stand, the more women go past, a parade of grease paint and crinolines.

A small hand takes mine, it's the lady dwarf. She tugs me forward and I feel myself pushed up the stairs as if carried by a tide, as though this small woman could support me. I follow the food. I follow the laughter and the flashes of blue flame belched by the fire-eater. I leave the dream.

The Story – Annie

When all that's left on our plates are crumbs and orange rinds, they teach me about the carnival. The aerialists and assistants are ordinary women. They are paid to hide rabbits in hats or hang from wires that they hold in their teeth, otherwise they are no different than me.

The freaks are born that way and make the best of what should be sorrow, Mariah's thick beard or Veronique's small stature.

The third group is geeks. Like the freaks, their attraction is rooted in their bodies, but not by fate. They have remade themselves, Lydia with her saffron hair and her body of tattoos, and Alice, who chews on glass and swallows fire.

But from where they sit tonight, I am the show, the melodrama unfolding of a respectable woman sliding into disrepute.

Alice returns from my room with my reticule and dumps the contents on the table. As the papers fall out, they push a red ball off the tabletop. I catch it in my hands. It feels spongy. I press down on the ball and a slit on the side gapes open at me. I realize it's a clown's nose.

"From the desk of Principal Reed, Santa Fe," Alice's brief introduction draws a cheer. "While a mature woman, and a widow, Mrs. Taylor nonetheless has a remarkable head for physical science. She is a woman of refinement and her ability to understand science does not make her any less respectable." They shout with laughter and Veronique refills my jelly jar with wine.

"Science doesn't make you less respectable, money does," Veronique says, "You know what people say about a working girl with her own money."

"Before I got my ink I was respectable—slaving as a maid for a dime a day. Now I make eight dollars a week!" Lydia tells me.

"In season," Veronique corrects her.

"But making money means I can't go to church without being read to from the pulpit by the minister," Lydia continues. Mariah snorts and returns the letter to me.

"We've seen you passing. A high necked collar and a long glove and you can't tell Lydia's inky at all," Mariah says.

I finger the gun that lies on the table. It's been recently fired. Sticking out of the barrel is a paper flag that reads "BANG!"

"Write down what can make you unrespectable and you'll have a book as thick as the Bible," Veronique says, climbing up into her chair. "You can't wear rouge. Or lip stain."

"You can't smoke," Mariah says as she lights a cheroot.

"When you dance, you need six inches between you and your fella," Alice adds.

"Oh, the Holy Spirit needs more room than that," Veronique corrects her, "at least ten."

"No holding hands, no kissing," Lydia says, tracing the wisteria vine that disappears into her sleeve.

"Not until you're betrothed," Veronique adds. "Because if you're caught—"

"—You don't have to be caught, the man can tell a story about you, he can just tell a story," Lydia says. Pink is rising from her collar.

"—Well then, you might as well run away and join the circus!" Veronique finishes.

They laugh and I'm surprised that there's no bitterness to their laughter. It flows as easily from them as foam slides down a beer glass. I tuck the paper flag back into the pistol.

"How did you end up here, Miss Annie?" Lydia asks. I owe them a song for my supper. I hold the gun to my head and tell my story.

"I'd rather be without brains than money," I say again, on my knees on the floor, my skirt gathered together in my hands. The women stare at me wide-eyed as I tell them how the knife flashed and the dress tore. I tell them how my life was stolen.

"Did you really say that?" Mariah asks.

"I'd finally saved enough money to retire. They took my life when they took my money," I tell them and put the pistol back on the table.

"That's a hell of a story," Veronique says and pulls a shawl around her shoulders.

"That's it!" Lydia shouts and claps her hands together, "Miss Annie could tell her story. People would pay to hear it."

I can't help myself, I laugh.

"I don't think any reasonable person would pay money to hear how I lost my pension."

"A new story. One they hadn't heard before. Remember, Mariah, last year in Chicago? There was a man who tried to climb Mount Everest. He called his lecture 'Journey to the Roof of the World.'"

"'Journey to the Fifth Floor of the World' was more like it. He didn't even make it half way!" Mariah snorts.

"Still, people paid good money to hear him talk," Lydia says, "A nickel a head."

"It's true," Veronique nods, "and they paid extra to see his missing toes. He lost three to frostbite. He had them in a jar." She shivers.

"I heard he cut his own toes off, so he could charge more money for his lecture," Mariah says and grinds out her cheroot in the plate of orange peels.

"I don't believe that!" Lydia says, "No one would ever cut themselves to make a dollar."

"Oh? Was that angel tattooed on your back?" Mariah asks. "Or was it painted on with a kitten's whiskers?"

Lydia throws a pillow at her.

"Don't tease her, Mariah," Veronique says, "Everyone knows those are birthmarks."

They laugh until tears run into Mariah's beard.

"Go ahead," Lydia says, standing up, "go ahead and laugh. But it's a great idea. Miss Annie could do something spectacular and still be respectable. Courage is a virtue, isn't it?" She turns to me and her blue eyes are bright with hope. "You could ski to the South Pole."

"I can't stand the cold—"

"—Or you could walk a tight rope over the Grand Canyon—"

"—I'm afraid of heights."

Lydia moves her chair to face me, our skirts touching at the knees. She takes my hand.

"You would need to find just one day, maybe just one hour of courage. Then for the rest of your life you could just talk about your amazing adventure," she is so serious, this laughing child. I want to ask her, what happened to you to make you choose a circus life. What was so bad, that carving pictures in the soft skin of your belly and arms was easier to bear? I want to ask, where did she find the courage? But all I can say is "How?"

"You get an agent, he books a hall, he charges tickets. Then you come out and tell the marks how you did the un-thinkable," she winds herself up, calling like a carnival barker, "the un-fathomable, the un-doable, un-believable feat!" She lowers her hands. "Then for an extra charge, you let them touch your skis or your tight rope. You could make twenty dollars a week."

My brain starts to whir, twenty dollars a week for talking. Teaching school I was making eight. But twenty? What could I do to make such a sum possible? She might as well tell me to head for the gold fields of Venezuela.

"Remember that fool who shot the Niagara Rapids last year?" Mariah asks, "He made a thousand dollars in one week at the World's Fair telling his story and showing off his barrel. And he didn't even go over the Falls, no one ever has."

A thousand dollars, that's almost the money I was going to retire on.

"I could earn a thousand dollars? Just by talking?" I ask.

"You'd need a big venue for that kind of take," Veronique says and tilts her head to one side. "The Pan-American Exposition opens in two weeks and runs through October. If you could make the closing week, you could make that kind of gate."

"So we need to get her to Buffalo, New York, in six week's time."

"A thousand dollars? Just for telling a story?" I ask again.

"With the right stunt. Something no one has ever tried before," Lydia reminds me.

"Better yet, a stunt no one has ever survived," Mariah corrects her. "If there were some well known failures or a couple of outright tragedies, that would sweeten your story."

"Either way, you'll have to prepare yourself for a life on the stage," Veronique says.

"I don't think I could ever wear paint," I tell them. As a child my mother had taken me to the opera in Chicago. I'd been frightened by the chalk white of the performers, the red slashes of their mouths.

"Perhaps," Veronique says and stands on a chair to look at me. She reaches up and lets down my braid, "But we must do something about your hair. If you're going to be a daredevil, you'll have to be a redhead."

I hold up my hand mirror. A red two shades short of brazen frames my eyes. I put the mirror back in my reticule. Can I change my life as easily as Veronique has changed my hair?

My fingers are swollen again this morning, puffing up on either side of my wedding ring. I spin the ring around my finger, pressing down the flesh before it. I slowly work it down towards the knuckle. It slides off onto the table, spins across the tabletop. I catch it in my hand as it rolls over the edge.

It is only a narrow band of gold, a few ounces, but still, my hand feels strangely light. I take a jar of salve from my reticule and rub it into my hands, working it into the joints the way I was instructed. There is no use putting the ring back on my finger.

I return to my problem, drawing the diagram in grease pencil on newspaper. It feels so familiar, to be alone in the gray morning with a calculation to draft. I never assigned a student a problem I hadn't solved myself first. I'd been fond of journey problems—a train moving east at 20 miles per hour passes a train moving west at 15.

I sketch out the height of Niagara Falls, the speed of the current, the weight of the water. Niagara Falls is less than a 100 miles from the Pan-American Exposition. If I could survive the Falls, I would have a story. I set for myself this problem to solve: how does a woman survive if she falls 200 feet locked in a barrel?

How does she survive if she doesn't?

THE NIAGARA FALLS

I sketch out the height of Niagara falls, the sound of the [illegible] the amount of the water. [illegible] feet and a [illegible] miles [illegible] the falls, I would [illegible] to give [illegible]

[illegible]

[illegible]

4   The Barrel – Annie

"The box will break you!" the man on the barrel shouts. He has drawn a crowd by standing on a barrel's spine and walking it back and forth beneath his feet. "A box has to be lifted, the barrel can be rolled. Any child could roll a barrel filled with five hundred pounds! The box must be stacked by a man and the box that cannot be lifted by a man will be lifted by a machine, and you will all be retired in favor of the forklift!"

I've heard sermons on mustard seeds of faith and vineyards of salvation, but never on the virtue of oak barrels. Standing on the barrel, Ivan Rozenski looks ten feet tall. I had tried to find him at his shop, he's the only cooper left in Saginaw. His apprentice led me here, to the crowded pier.

"This cask holds 100 lbs. of bourbon and any woman, any child could move it. I say any woman! Any child!"

"Care to put money on it?" a dockworker shouts. He holds a black iron hook used to spear bales of cotton. His shirt is plastered to him with exertion.

"I'll do better than that, *pfeife*. If I'm wrong I'll tap this keg!" The crowd cheers. "Volunteer! I need a volunteer!" the cooper shouts. Fishmongers and dockworkers rush forward.

"I can do it," I shout, but I'm drowned out. Bring the class to order, bring them in from the playground, "I can do it!" I shout as loud as I ever have. If I win this bet for him he will listen to me, he must.

He jumps down from the barrel and the crowd parts before him till he's towering over me. Behind him comes the barrel, rolled by another apprentice, a twelve-year old boy in a leather apron. In a minute, the barrel is righted. I hand Mr. Rozenski my reticule and he shoves it at the boy.

"She starts here!" he shouts and paces down the dockside. From his pocket he produces a wedge of chalk. "She ends here!" It's a space about twenty feet long. I put my hands on the barrel rim and grip it tightly. It comes to the middle of my chest.

"Stand back!" he shouts and the crowd retreats, creating a corridor.

I push my weight against the barrel. It is heavy but it rocks slightly forwards. I lean back pulling it with me. The crowd is waiting, willing me to fail. I rock it forward again and it rises up on its edge. Quickly, I move to the side, the barrel on its edge now leaning into me. Together we turn.

I shuffle it to the right, then the left, turning it around and around in my hands. It's a bulky dance partner, throwing its weight around. I struggle to keep it balanced, keep it moving. My face is hot. I can feel my shift growing damp. Ten feet left to go, eight feet. I'm panting. The crowd seems to hiss, with my every step the promised liquor is draining away. Five feet to go. A spot between my shoulders starts to burn. Three feet.

"This delicate creature could move the world if it were packaged in a barrel!" Mr. Rozenski shouts.

Two. One. Cheers! The crowd cheers, for me. I've done it! They forgive me for disappointing them, for stealing their drink. My hands are cramping and I let the barrel go too soon. It doesn't rock to standing, but forward, over, down off the edge of the dock, into the Saginaw River. The splash comes up and washes over my boots.

"*Quatsch!*" the cooper shouts.

"Salvage!" comes a cry from the crowd and I'm thrown back as men rush for the edge of the dock, reaching into the water for the barrel. Mr. Rozenski and his apprentice race forward and I open my mouth to apologize. The apprentice holds out my reticule and Ivan slaps the bag from his hands. He lifts the boy by the collar and throws him into the river.

"Bring me the barrel!" he shouts as the boy's head breaks the water, gasping from the cold. The cooper spits, turns on his heel, and leaves, the crowd parting before him.

Half an hour later, I follow the apprentice into the shop. I paid a dime to have a dockworker fish him out. He was clinging to the barrel like it was the wreck of the Hesperus.

The shop smells of sawdust. My damp boots shuffle the wood curls as I follow the dripping boy into the back. Ivan Rozenski is sitting with his back to me, running a two-handled lathe along a piece of wood.

"Mr. Rozenski?" I ask. He looks over his shoulder.

"Out!" he shouts, dropping the lathe. "Out before you destroy something else!"

"I beg your pardon, I just won you a bet," my cheeks are hot.

"You just put a barrel of bourbon in the Saginaw!"

"And I paid to fish it out, the barrel and the boy!" He hasn't even noticed the boy dripping at my elbow.

"*Gott in Himmel*, woman— "

"—Mrs. Taylor," I hold my hand out to him.

"Hurricanes also have names," he says and turns back to his bench. "Enough dripping, Hans! Change!" he yells over his shoulder and the wet boy scuffs off leaving a trail of water through the sawdust.

I walk around the room, past the wood lined up against the wall, the stacks of iron rings. The bench he straddles slopes away from him. He has a small black iron ring balanced against the wood and he's filling it with staves, placing them together like jigsaw puzzle pieces. It's a small ring for a small cask, the kind molasses is sold in.

"I need a barrel," I tell him.

"They were listening," he mutters, sliding another stave into the ring. "They were seeing the truth about the box and then you! With one touch! *Quatsch!*"

Blood is pounding in my ears. If I'm to make the Pan-American Exposition, I have to have the barrel before I leave for New York. There can be no delay. He has to help me.

"Would you be interested in proving, scientifically proving, that there are some jobs for which only a barrel will suffice? And to use anything other than a barrel would mean disaster?" I'm talking too fast, I'm rattling on. "Don't you think that would be good for your business?" He doesn't even look up.

"As long as there's a need for bourbon, I'll have a living. You can't age bourbon in a cardboard box."

I fumble with my bag and pull out my newspaper clippings. I've pieced them together with straight pins.

"Over the last three years, fifteen people have announced their intention to go over Niagara Falls, to conquer it. Each daredevil used a different contraption, all of which were destroyed in the attempt," I hold the clippings out to him.

"I've no need to read your coupons," he snarls.

"One man was foolish enough to consider going over in a box!" That's a lie but I have to make him listen.

"A box!" the name of his enemy causes him to explode. "*Verdammit noch mal!*" he yells, kicking a stave across the floor.

"I think you'll agree that even reinforced with steel a box would collapse. A right angle can't absorb the impact of that kind of fall," I hold out the clippings again. He takes them, he's scowling but he takes them.

"What do these fools have to do with me?" he asks, flipping through the articles.

"I believe a person could survive going over Niagara Falls if they went over in a barrel," I tell him. He laughs.

"I have no intention of going over Niagara Falls, Mrs. Taylor."

"But I do," I say quickly, "I mean to go over Niagara Falls in one of your barrels."

"*Quatsch,*" he replies. He looks me up and down, then hands me back my clippings. Hans returns, shivering but dry.

"Tap the barrel, Hans," Ivan tells him.

"Sir?" the boy asks, looking back and forth between us.

"Tap it *pfeife*! Bring me a glass! And bring the lady a doctor, she's lost her mind!" he sits back at his bench, muttering.

"I'm not mad," I tell him, though I know that's exactly what a mad woman would say. "I'm a science teacher and I've applied everything I know to solving the problem of the Falls." I pull out my plans and unfold them. He doesn't move when I lay the paper on the bench before him.

"If you look at this calculation, here is the height of Niagara Falls…here is the angle of the fall, the weight of the water, the weight of the barrel…it is possible to survive. I know it. I can prove it, but I need your help."

"Help to kill yourself, you mean? Hans! Where's my drink?" he shouts.

"A million people will visit the Pan-American Exposition in Buffalo, New York this October. Every booth of inventions, every musical revue, they're each guaranteed an audience of 30,000 people. That's a minimum of 30,000 people who learn that the barrel is the only thing that can, the only thing that ever will, survive Niagara Falls." I see him hesitate.

"You can guarantee 30,000 people?" he asks.

"And I'll tell every single one of them that Ivan Rozenski made the barrel that conquered Niagara Falls," I finish, raising my voice when I say his name. Lydia had made me practice this rise and fall of the sentence, this singsong. She called it "the pitch."

"Why? Why would you do this?" he asks.

"For the price of admission. These 30,000 people, their tickets will give me back my life," I tell him.

"If you live to see it. No husband?" He asks, "No family?"

I nod. There is no use explaining how black of a sheep I've become, how my gentile starvation would please my brother, how my survival would defy him.

Ivan turns to the barrels that line the walls and gestures at them with his glass of bourbon.

"If you ride in one of these barrels you'll flip end over end until your spine cracks. You'll be dead in the river before you fall. You need a custom job, something designed to keep you upright in the water."

"I couldn't agree more, my design requires the barrel to have uneven ends, wider at the top than at the bottom. This will trap oxygen near my head," I can see he's listening to me. He's considering it. I'm dizzy with hope and my hands cramp as I try to dig the plans out of my bag.

"A pint glass, I make it like a pint glass," he says, "The Pan-American Exposition is in October—that's two days to make a custom barrel. Hans! Bring me a pint glass!"

"I took the liberty of making you a template," I say and manage to unfold the ivory tissue without tearing it. I lay it open on the workbench. He touches the paper and the moisture on his fingertips causes it to stick to him.

"*Wott* is this? Tissue?" he asks.

"It's a dress pattern. For the barrel."

"Dress pattern! *Himmel arsch and zwirn!*" he shakes his hand to get the paper off, it tears and he crumples it into a ball.

I rub my left thumb against the back of my ring finger. That nervous gesture had worn my wedding band thin, it had cost me in the price at the pawnbrokers.

"I pawned my wedding ring for this," I tell him.

"Pawned? Not sold?" he asks.

"I'm going to return from Niagara Falls and I'm going to get my ring back," I tell him. "That's a promise."

He's silent, staring. He leans in close to me.

"Done!" he shouts and spits into his open palm. I grasp his hand like a woman drowning. "We need Kentucky oak, it makes the strongest staves. Hans!" he shouts and begins tearing through his stock.

I sink down onto his bench. I struggle to control my breath, I don't want him to hear how ragged it is. I don't want him to see my hands tremble.

The barrel is shorter than I am, just a bit over four feet. I'll have to crouch inside it. It's wrapped in black iron bands every eight inches. The base seems delicate under the wide shoulders of the lid.

I put my hand to the wood. Ivan had me choose each stave myself. I think he meant to test my resolve by having me choose the wood for what could become my coffin.

"It will resist 2,000 pounds of pressure from the inside," he says proudly, as if it matters.

"How much pressure can it bear from the outside?" I ask.

"Ten times that number," he says, "The staves are carved like keystone joints—you could stand an elephant on the outside and the barrel wouldn't crack."

I nod. I've taught lessons on keystone joints. To illustrate the principle I'd had my students create arches of stone they could sit on without collapsing. The boys had deliberately set up arches they knew would fail, they delighted in tumbling into the dust.

"Now," Ivan says as he tips the barrel onto its side, "let's test it." He tips it forward so that the wide mouth of the barrel gapes at me, ready to swallow me whole. I remove my hat, sliding the pin back through the felt before placing it on the workbench. I lower myself to the ground in front of the barrel. Ivan braces it so it doesn't roll and I crawl backwards until my boots are inside. Then there's the matter of my skirt.

I look up. Ivan and Hans are staring at me. I frown best "eyes on your own paper," and they both look away, then up. I pull my skirt up to my knees and shimmy into the barrel.

"You'll have to find someone to launch the barrel," Ivan says to the ceiling. "The lid has to be banged into place from the outside with a mallet. Then the lid needs to be secured with an iron ring. Do you understand me? If you don't add the last ring, when you hit the river, the top of the barrel will fly off. The Falls will crush you before you can drown."

I need someone with a mallet, and a boat upriver to tow me midstream. I need someone to cast me into the river. If I try to launch from the riverbank, I risk beaching myself on the banks above the Falls.

I need someone downriver to fish me out. Someone to break off the last ring, someone to free me. I have to find these people and then convince them I'm not mad.

"Would you come to Niagara with me? I would pay you," I ask.

"Any man with a hammer can help you. What you need now is a manager, someone to start the money machine. If you don't get somebody to handle the money, then you'll have risked your life for nothing."

Lydia had told me the same thing. The money is in the story, the trick is getting someone to pay to hear it. A manager would find an audience, fill the seats, charge the tickets. I need to find someone who knows how to make my fall pay.

"I'm ready," I tell Ivan and together he and Hans raise the barrel upright. The base is only twice the width of my feet. My skirt pools around my waist and I tuck it down with my hands. Ivan looks down at me and frowns. I must look like I'm melting into the fabric.

"How does it feel?" he asks.

"Like a pair of very heavy shoes," I reply.

He holds up the lid in his left hand. It's two inches thick, designed to fit the barrel snug enough to prevent any water from reaching me.

"Shall we begin," he asks, as if this were a dance. I feel as if I'm staring up at him from the bottom of a well. I nod. He lowers the lid into place.

It's like a total eclipse of the sun and I sink into blackness. The barrel trembles as the mallet pounds the lid into place. I hear the clang of iron, the steel wedge forcing the last ring down. I press my hands to the underside of the lid. No thread of light comes in, no hint of air.

I had stayed in the room when they put the lid on my baby's coffin. I'd been advised to leave by the doctor, by David, but I fought to stay. Then I fought to push the lid back. Scratched and bit as the lid was lowered and hammered into place. The coffin was so small, hardly bigger than the cradle he'd just outgrown.

Bang!

The thin edge of a chisel is thrust under the lid and there's a crack of light. The lid pops off. I squint and gasp as air rushes into the barrel.

Ivan reaches down, grabs me under the arms and pulls me up. I'm gasping, sucking air as if I'd been underwater. My legs have cramped up, I struggle to straighten them. I try to control my breathing. The heat, the closeness of the barrel, has caused me to sweat. I wipe my forehead with the back of my hand.

A lilac scented glove offers me a handkerchief. I turn to face Lydia. Just as Mariah had said, she is passing amongst the regular town folk in a long glove and a high collar. She's smiling, but there's a deep 'V' of worry between her brows. I try to thank her, but no sound comes out. The edges of her face fade into shadow.

"*Quatsch!*" Ivan shouts and catches me before I swoon. He carries me to the bench below the window and Lydia fans me as he throws it open. The dockside smell of fish fills my nostrils, replacing the smell of wood. I clutch the sill, shaking. I squeeze my eyes tightly shut, try to force away the feeling of a tight, close space, the feeling of a coffin.

"How long?" I ask. Ivan checks his pocket watch.

"53 minutes. Maybe an hour of air. After that, you'll start to choke."

I had never considered suffocation. I can't stop trembling. I try to think of the formula for measuring the volume of a gas. The oxygen in the barrel dwindling as each exhalation poisons the air.

"One hour, it can't take that long to fall," Lydia says, and I know she's struggling to encourage me. She digs into her bag and pulls out a piece of paper, "I found an agent for you! He manages trick high divers, even the kind that dives on horseback. I figure he's a natural to help you. When you go over Niagara Falls, you'll be the highest diver anyone's ever seen."

I look at the name, Frank M. Russell, Talent Agent. Here is the help I need, to get the boat captains and the porters and the press. I will have to send him a cable, to meet me in Niagara. I think of the telegraph office, the tap of the keys, the words arranged to sell him on me, and the barrel and the Falls. I focus on each step ahead and slowly the darkness of the barrel recedes and my heartbeat begins to slow. The fall can be done. It must.

Newlyweds – Annie

I finger the cable from Frank M. Russell. I've folded and unfolded it so many times that I fear it will begin to tear. He has taken on the job. He is priming the pump in Boston, New York and Philadelphia. New York alone has twelve daily papers. If the newsmen can make it to Buffalo, he's promised a private train car will take them to Niagara.

I have faith in Mr. Russell. His every word assures me that there's an audience. But a part of me rankles at his promises, the same part that used to chase water diviners from the front porch when I lived in New Mexico.

"*Pfeife!*" Ivan curses as the apprentice shuffles the barrel towards the baggage car. I'm grateful that he swears only in

German. The words are like the steam of the train whistle, sharp and startling, but harmless.

I watch the other passengers as they hand their luggage off to the porters and collect their tickets. My own ticket is one-way, second-class. I declined to purchase a round trip ticket. Either I'll return first class, or not at all.

"Lord, don't they have newlywed written all over them," Lydia laughs and points her chin at a young couple on the platform. They are barely older than some of my students and it is clear their clothes are new purchases, they look stiff and contained. The young man says something to the young woman, tipping his hat as he does so. There's a cascade of rice and the bride blushes and steps forward so that her skirt covers the grains.

"I've secured the barrel," Ivan says. He looks dressed for church in a suit, cap in hand.

"Thank you for believing in me," I tell him and hold out my hand. In a second I'm aloft, squeezed in a bear hug, and then dropped back on the platform.

"I've something for you," Ivan says and takes from his pocket a worn $5 bill. "There's bookies in Niagara. I want you to place a bet on yourself."

"Respectable women don't gamble," I tell him.

"*Quatsch!*" Ivan shouts and Lydia puts her glove to her mouth to keep from laughing. "You're a respectable woman and you're gambling with your life." He turns to Lydia, and takes her red cheeks as alarm. "If she were going over in a box, she'd be coming home in a coffin. But she's going over in my barrel and she's going to be just fine." Lydia can't help herself then, she laughs like a bell ringing and nods her head in agreement.

Minutes later I am looking down at them from the window of the passenger car. They are not quite side-by-side, standing stiffly, as if they were resisting a tide tugging them towards one another. The whistle blows, the engine lurches forward and the wheels of the passenger cars slowly start to turn. I wave my handkerchief at them from the open window.

I am sharing a car with the newlyweds. Or I will be. Right now it is just the groom, silent and distracted, on the bench seat across from me. He runs the band of his hat through his fingers, staring at the floor.

I realize I've been clutching my reticule tightly, the tension of my grip has caused my hands to ache. I remove my gloves. My left hand looks strangely naked without my ring. I open my reticule and reach for my salve.

The door to the car opens and the bride enters. The groom jumps to his feet and the bride stumbles forward, unable to negotiate her new traveling dress. He holds his arms out for her stiffly and they seem to bounce off one another before falling into the seat. They stare at each other, unable to look away. I lower my head and work the liniment into the joints of my fingers. They are both so young. Could they even be twenty? How young was I? Seventeen?

"If you'll excuse me," the groom says loudly, as if announcing the time. He stands and leaves the car.

I watch the girl for a moment. She twists her hands around the handle of her bag and pulls at the side of her shirtwaist. She looks like she's waiting to go on stage in an unfamiliar costume, an understudy Gibson Girl. I can't help but smile, last year she was probably still following Dorothy's adventures in Oz.

"Congratulations," I say and she stiffens. "You were married today, weren't you?"

"How can you tell?" she asks and her cheeks have gone red.

"Husbands don't tip their hats to their wives," I tell her and her shoulders slump. "And you're leaving a trail of rice."

She withdraws her hatpin from her hat and gently shakes the last grains of rice out onto the floor of the car.

"I don't want people to know," she says, "When people know you're newlyweds, they fall all over themselves and they tease you and they wink. They wink a lot at Malcolm."

I remember that feeling, that everyone knew what you were up to but you. And even worse, the guilty knowledge that what you did together in your bedroom was done by the people around you with their old, imperfect bodies.

"If you don't want to look like newlyweds, you'll have to start taking your husband for granted," I say.

"Oh, I could never do that."

"It can be as simple as not looking at him when he speaks. You stare at each other as if you've discovered a new country."

"Where should I look?" the bride asks.

"Just not at him. If he hands you something, don't look at him when you accept it," I tell her. She nods and I can see she is working this over in her mind.

The door slides open and Malcolm returns, holding his hat and a small brown paper bag. She keeps her eyes on the window and the slaking fields. He shifts his feet from one foot to the other, waiting. She doesn't look at him.

"I bought you a packet of peanuts," he says. I watch as the bride turns her shoulder slightly away from him, "I thought you liked peanuts." She holds out her hand without turning her head and he hands her the peanuts, looking hurt and confused. I feel sorry for him, my bright idea to put her at ease has made him miserable. He sits and sullenly scuffs at the rice on the floor.

I excuse myself and as I slide the door open, I hear the bride whisper to him.

"Stop looking at me."

"But I like looking at you," he says.

I can't help myself, I turn to look at them as I close the door behind me. She has turned to him and they are staring into each other's eyes. I put my hand to my mouth and stifle a laugh. This is the greatest difficulty they have—being too obviously in love. I remember that and now I'm trying not to cry.

Lift – Bicycle Boy

"The lovers come a thousand miles
They leave their homes and mothers
But when they reach Niagara Falls
They only see each other."

Grooms and brides, grooms and brides, two by two, like animals leaving the ark. There's a trick to skimming them. Take a young man with a young bride, he won't notice if your hand dips quick into his pocket. The wallets come easy but the pickings are slim. Young grooms book the boarding houses and the budget views of the Falls.

The real take is May/December. An old man with a child bride is paying top dollar all the way. Table Rock. The Cascade Hotel. But fat wallets are shoved deep down. The grooms keep one hand on the leather. They know the fat wallet is how they got their child bride. It's a hard lift, but I have the bike.

"Bicycles to rent! Sterlings of the finest steal! Safe for Woman or Child! See the Niagara Gorge astride the Finest Flyers!"

Done! It's near a half inch thick with a feel like a rabbit's ear. Burke will be happy with this one.

I loop back. There's a woman, alone.

Lone lady travelers usually get off stateside, fanatics for Dr. Kellogg's sanatorium. They're heading for horse feed and milk curds three times a day, there's not a sightseer among them.

"Miss! Miss! Rent a bicycle! Bathe in air! Bathe in sunshine! Ride a gentle mare made of steel! Safe for Woman or Child!" I shout.

"Please, fetch me a porter," she says and her look goes straight to my backbone till I'm standing in the pedals. Then I see what she's watching.

Mr. Davis always says "you learn about people by watching what they watch." So I watch what she's watching. Not the carpet bag at her feet, I could lift that and take it away on my head. She's watching a barrel, standing on the platform with the trunks and tagged for delivery.

Mr. Davis says "There's two kinds of trouble at the Falls, jumpers and stunters, and both are bad for business." Seems both kinds see the water falling and go loose limbed, ready to drop. For Mr. Davis half the trouble of booking a stunter is keeping them alive long enough to open the book on them. "You've got to watch 'em," he says, "cause if people can't place a bet on a stunter's death, that's a tragedy."

I've seen stunters like that myself, but this woman's all wrong. She's too straight for a stunter and too cool for a jumper. But that barrel...that worries me. I'd best leave her to Burke.

I find him in the circle of hackmen down beside the departures throwing dice. When he hears my bell, he puts out his hand for the wallet without looking up. His palm is as wide across as a baseball mitt. I drop the wallet into it.

"There's a woman got off the train, alone, with a barrel," I say and the hack chatter quiets.

"What ya think, Burke? Another Maude Willard?" one asks, "Davis expecting another Maude?"

But Burke is up and gone, straight through the dice and the stakes, the hackmen scrambling away from him, fumbling for the coins in the dirt.

"What's the bet on another Maude?" I hear someone call and I take after Burke to see how he handles this trouble.

The Egg – The Porter

Will you look at it? Bright with new wood. Nine rings round it, that's a fine waste of iron when every porter knows you need no more 'n five.

Train's in all day with barrels, full up with pickles or flour or bourbon. I tip them and I kick them and I bear walk them down the platform. Roll them to the hackmen and collect me tip. But when I kicked this one, didn't it spin back, chop me in the knee and like to cripple me? The cursed thing, uneven, one end like a cart wheel, the other like a Sunday bonnet.

"I'm afraid you'll have to stand the barrel on its edge and shimmy it down the platform," says she, "The larger side is the top of the barrel."

So I walk it on the small edge. Turn round and round with the wide end between my arms. And it makes me feel queer, like I'm dancing a stout woman in circles. Then the charlatans arrive on the dance floor.

"Madam, let me show you Niagara! Queen of the Cataracts! The Water Bride of Time! The Daughter of History! The Mother of all Waterfalls! Hear the fateful story of the Maid of the Mist, the Indian Maiden who journeyed through death to be transformed into mist!" sings the man at her right.

"Niagara! The lure for daredevils everywhere! Tour the sights of daring! The Great Blondin who crossed Niagara on a wire! Learn the secrets of the funambulists who crossed the Niagara Gorge. William Campbell, who surged the Niagara Rapids in a barrel! See the Niagara Whirlpool!" sings the man at her left.

"Whirlpool?" she asks. "What whirlpool?" But they're gone and that means something's coming, something with claws.

I turn the barrel again and there's Burke, his finger pointing at the barrel and his gesture means "that's all mine." Up goes the barrel, onto his back and he's off! Taking the barrel, taking the woman, taking the tip as well!

"I need a coach to Arrow Street," she says to Burke, no she shouts it to his back. She has to lift her skirts to follow him fast enough. Look at her, you can see the very tops of her boots!

Arrow Street. She'll be wanting the boarding house, but that's not where he's taking her. It's fair trade, kidnapping guests and some say that's Burke's specialty. He gives penalties to guests that fail to drop their kings and presidents at Mr. Davis's attractions. Burke upends them, shakes them, takes the last coins that fall from their pockets.

Well, Burke has the woman now, and he'll make straight for Mr. Davis. He'll keep the little woman and her egg of a barrel. I bet Mr. Forsyth will pay me the stolen tip to know of her.

Siren – Annie

I could not see the Falls from the train. The bridge crosses upriver and all I could see was a flat expanse of water and a plume of white rising into the air. It's a column of mist, easily two stories high, thrown into the air when the water crashes on the rocks. It looks like a magic lantern show I saw once about Old Faithful.

I could not see the Falls from the train station. I suppose this is partly for the safety of the rails. Certainly, it benefits the merchants. Everyone must travel back from the tracks towards the river to spend their money.

I watch the man secure my barrel and then climb into the carriage. Over the wheels of the coach I hear a sound, a rumble, like a train approaching, but with no variance, a train that neither speeds up nor slows down. The rumble becomes thunder. We are getting closer.

We stop, but the coach continues to vibrate. It trembles from the wheels up. My mouth floods with the taste of tin. That thunder—it must be the Falls.

The man doesn't open the door. He takes the barrel down first and I feel the coach shift as the weight of it is released. He starts to walk away, my barrel on his shoulder.

I grab my bag and get out. It's raining. No, not rain, but mist falling like rain. I look for the sound, but the Table Rock Hotel is a three-story barrier, with high walls on either side. They've made the view of the Falls a condition of checking in.

I follow the man. In the lobby, centered beneath a chandelier, is a fountain. It's the Horseshoe Falls in miniature, curving three feet from end to end with a basin cluttered with copper pennies.

"I am not a guest of the Table Rock Hotel," I try not to shout, but my heart is pounding. This place I can't afford. He puts the barrel down and then holds up his hand to silence me. He hears something and then I hear it. It's a siren.

"Man overboard," he says and leaves me with the barrel. I watch him push through a set of double doors on the opposite wall. With them open, the siren is louder.

Man overboard! They can't mean someone in the river heading for the Falls. I start to run. I join the rush of maids, hackmen and guests. I'm pushed through a dark dining room towards a sliver of gray sky in the verandah's doorway.

And I see the Falls.

I grew up beside Lake Huron. Here it is again, only this time, tipped on its edge and draining down through a narrow chasm. Here Lake Huron is falling with Erie, Michigan, Ontario and Superior.

I blink and a million gallons of water fall before me. I blink again and another million goes over the edge. I shiver. Every hair on my body is standing on end.

"Where is he?" I ask the man who stole my barrel. I scan the river above the Falls, but I can't see anyone.

"If you could see him, he'd already be dead," is all the man says. Everything we can see of the river above the Falls is already the point of no return.

I hear a muttering, like someone praying. I wish it were a prayer. I wish I was praying for the man overboard, but it's me repeating over and over like a crow cawing.

This is a bad idea.

This is a bad idea.

This is a very bad idea.

Overboard – Maude

Tell it true. Not a man overboard, but a woman. And not overboard. Not yet.

A mile upriver of the Falls, on the New York side, there's an inlet, an oxbow off the main current. Go there and you can rent a rowboat and explore a lazy afternoon. There the water's nearly still.

It's rare that any man is rash enough to row a rented boat into the main current of the river. More rare for that same fool to lose his grip on one of his oars. And it takes a true imbecile to lean so far over to get it back that he falls into the river himself.

The woman screaming in the rowboat, she's married to such a jackass.

Now, a man finding himself with one oar, coasting downstream, knowing where the ride's taking him—a man would have jumped overboard and tried to swim for shore.

But a woman in a wool gabardine dress, a bride with pearl buttons up the back, she knows that's the quickest way to die, being dragged to the bottom as the wet wool becomes an anchor. No, better for her to flail with the remaining oar and scream for a last chance. Scream for someone to help her.

For there's other boats docked upriver. Ferries for those too frightened by Niagara's suspension bridge to cross it. Can you blame them? Look at it! No center pylons, no support, nothing that touches the ground beneath the water. It hangs by wires and it sways in the wind. It's like crossing a cobweb. And to top it off, you share that bridge with the train. Anyway you put it, the Niagara Bridge sounds like a bar bet. Folks are right to feel afraid of it.

Fear of those wires keeps John Stilwell and his boat in business, ferrying folks from Niagara to Niagara, Canada to New York. So you could say fear is going to give that woman her last chance.

It's the hydro-dam workers that set off the alarm. They're building above the Falls. The alarm is set up for them. More than a few have fallen to the river. Half have been lucky.

When he heard the siren, Stilwell kicked off his boots. Like a dog hearing his master's whistle, he kicked 'em off before he even turned to face the river.

Before he even saw the bride, he was in the water, a towrope in his teeth. Swimming straight across, heading for America, aiming to cut her off.

The bride's given up on the oar, but not on her screaming. She's decided to make a swim for it. Wrestling with her dress. Those pearl buttons, a dime a pop, fall to the bottom of the boat.

Pop! Pop! Pop!

Oh that'll be better for the press. Let her be stripped to her white cotton bloomers, her loose hair cascading down her back, standing in the boat as she skates towards hell. They'll always remember her then—the dam workers that are watching from the bluffs, the tourists that have stopped their coaches on the bridge, the picnickers watching through coin operated telescopes.

If not for the roar of the Falls, their voices would carry to the bride. She can't hear them, but I do.

"I've got a dollar says she's done for!"

Make the cutoff, Stilwell.

"Two says she makes it!"

Make the cutoff.

"There's a man in the water! He's swimming for her!"

Make the cutoff.

"I say they both go over, anyone?! Anyone?!"

Every stroke he takes to cross the river, the river pushes him down towards the Falls and—

He's got her! He grabs the stern of the boat and now it's dragging them both towards the edge. He's shouting something to her, they've only seconds to act.

Take the rope, woman! Doing what you're told may be what got you here, but damn it, do what you're told! Tie the wet rope around your waist. Climb slowly into the water. Trust him and lie still as a corpse on your back. Even as the current tries to push you both towards hell, don't try to swim.

Trust him and you just might be saved.

The Charm – Davis

When the charm walks in, the marks barely give her a glance. She doesn't look like a chance to change your luck. Auburn curls that might have been true at twenty and now are too bright to be real. Those curls and her ostrich feather hat, they're worth considering.

I don't have to tell you that there are scholars at Saratoga watching for clues to the next scratch. They track the bloodlines, and the oat choices, and they know which mares favor the mud. Every detail examined for a hint at which stallion will win, every horse under their eye. But you see, I watch people, and from what I can see, this charm is in it up to her neck.

"Please, do come in," I call. I place my hand on the barrel, my cigar smoldering. The pose says to her, your luggage is my ashtray. She gives me a look of pure rage. No hatred, no fear. Now let's see her handle the room.

"A tourist arrives at Niagara Falls with one bag and one big, empty, barrel," I say it louder than the table games. Some of the marks put their cards face down on the felt and turn to look her over. I give them just a hint of heat. "I take it you're planning a very short, very steep trip, Mrs. Taylor," and I give a draw to my cigar.

"How do you know my name?" is all the charm says. I nod at Burke. He tips the barrel forward so the marks can see the packing label. I read it to them.

"Property of Mrs. Annie E. Taylor, Saginaw, Michigan."

No word from her, just gray eyes straight at mine.

"I'm Saul Davis, the proprietor of the Table Rock Hotel, Niagara's finest accommodation," I begin but I can see the details of the many luxuries available here are making her wrinkle.

"This is not a hotel—it's a den of thieves," she sparks, "I demand you return the barrel to me." A good laugh line for the marks and they take it. Look at them, they each think they're a thief, stealing from chance, stealing from the house, stealing from me. They're children.

"So when are you going over the Falls?" I ask.

"Over?" a mark asks, "You mean she's not another Maude?" The room is starting to hum. They're just back at their cards, most of them left to bet on the fate of the man in the river. When he never appeared at the brink of the foam, they went back to the felt.

"Not a Maude boys, Mrs. Taylor is aiming for the Big One. She's taking this barrel over Niagara Falls," and I slap the top of the barrel with my palm. It thumps like a drum and the hum from the marks grows louder—"what's the book," they're wondering, "when does it open?"

"This is no business of yours," the charm says, but she hasn't moved. No advance and no retreat. Not a bad sign.

"Everything that happens in Niagara is my business. Or at least half of it is," I admit.

"Right you are, Mr. Davis, fifty, fifty," a mark calls. I'll see about that.

Look at the charm, she's blushing! She wanted a conversation and what she's got is a performance. There's nothing Maude about her, no interest in the stage.

"I'll go over in two days time," she says as if announcing the date of a church social.

"That doesn't leave enough time for publicity, make it a week," and I give Beade a nod. The paper man scribbles. Tomorrow's paper will be about the save. I imagine there'll be a photograph of the waterlogged woman and the riverman. Never follow a save with a fall, that's my motto. Give me a week and she can follow a disaster.

"No, if I wait a week it will be my birthday," the charm says.

"How many candles?" I ask.

"Thirty nine? Again?" comes a call.

"And again and again and again," answers the room. I never said they were gentlemen.

"A fall on your birthday—I like it, it sells," I clap my hands and Beade scribbles. "Here's the play. You go over on your birthday, if you survive, you celebrate at the Table Rock Hotel. We have a big cake, make it the shape of the barrel—we fill the Horseshoe Fountain with champagne."

"Your photo runs in every newspaper in the U.S. and Canada. You, the barrel and the Table Rock Hotel. A series of photographs right in front of the fountain in the lobby. You endorse the Table Rock Hotel in every interview. You endorse it fully."

"I don't understand," she interrupts Beade's dictation, "You want me to be a guest here?"

"Only if you survive. We can't have you stay here until after you fall. If you die while staying here—that's bad advertising and bad business." I snap at Beade. "Till you fall, there's a boarding house, the Oxford, you'll stay there."

"I have a reservation with Mrs. Alice Johnson on Arrow Street," she says and I wave her off.

"You'll stay at the Oxford for your own protection. From the police while you put your crazy stunt into action," I tell her. If possible, she stands even straighter.

"I'm not crazy. I'm a respectable woman," and those words do the marks in. They laugh till they would burst. They all know a tradeswoman who claims respectability.

I gesture to Burke. I don't want my words getting lost in their jeers. He barely turns his head towards the marks and they are suddenly silent.

"It's illegal to go over the Falls, Mrs. Taylor," I explain. "It's considered suicide and the law says murder is a crime even if you're only killing yourself." I cross the room to her. "Now you can take your barrel, and you can leave and try to fall without me. But I'll bet every man in this room you'll be in jail or Thornhill Asylum before you can reach the riverbank."

I can see this is news to her. Stunters—they all think it's just them and the water, but it's a business.

"You giving odds on that, Mr. Davis?" one of the marks asks, then bolts from the room when he sees Burke shift his weight. Really, they're like mice.

"Take my protection and I promise you'll fall," I tell her and then I wait. Now spinsters, they're known for being desperate graspers at chance. But in my experience, widows are cooler customers because they've dispensed with hope.

"I am not committing suicide," Mrs. Taylor says.

"That remains to be seen," I tell her, and this time the room is silent.

"What kind of protection would you offer?" she asks me.

"Ab," I say and he steps forward. That single step usually cows the marks and the twists. Ab's mother named her three sons after the American Emancipator —Abraham, Abe and Ab. As their names got shorter, the brothers got larger.

"Ab's your hackman and your body guard. He'll keep you safe until you fall," I say and Beade scribbles some more. And the charm, this is what she does.

"Ab," she says and holds out her little hand in her little cotton glove to say "how-de-do" to him.

"Miss Annie," says he, like it's goddamn Sunday social time. The marks don't know what to make of it. Beade stops his scribbling.

"If you could bring the barrel, I'd like to go now, Ab," she says and she turns for the door.

"The barrel stays here!" I can't help but shout. "Ab, put it in the front window. I want velvet ropes to keep the folks in the lobby back. I want a guard." Later I'll tell Beade to get a shill to pester that guard, someone who'll demand to inspect the barrel. We need to start building some excitement. A good shill at work in a packed lobby, you could fry an egg in the time it would take for the paying guests to start pestering the guard to let them closer to the barrel, too.

"You got an agent?" I ask.

"Frank Russell, he arrives tomorrow on the train," Mrs. Taylor says.

"Fine. When Russell arrives," I tell Ab, "Bring him to me. Keep Forsyth and his flunky's away from her."

Ab knows it's time to leave. Every mark is eyeing the charm, weighing her as a twist. They think they know how to handicap a stunter.

They're wrong.

11 Stunters – Ab

Hear the door close and the book open. Mr. Davis calls it the "chicken bet." Will the stunter go over? Or turn chicken and run?

It's the same for every stunter. A mark sees all that water falling and he starts to shrink. He figures the stunter feels the same, that he'll turn tail and leave. My job is to see they don't. If you come to the Falls and sign with Mr. Davis, you'll fall all right. I make it a sure thing.

But make no mistake, this ain't Isaac I'm tying to the rock. No, the trick with a stunter is to keep them from falling without a crowd. They're prone to melancholia, need the Falls to lift their spirits, need the dare to make the next day. Mr. Davis says "no one wants catastrophe when they've paid for tragedy." So I sit on them till Mr. Davis has the press and the audience and the book. Then I let them be. And they fall.

"Ab, is Mr. Forsyth the sheriff?" Miss Annie asks. She's been watching the installation of the barrel like a mama hen over a chick.

"No, ma'am," I answer, "He's a businessman, like Mr. Davis." And for most who come to Niagara, that's all he is. Just another suit, another name on the brass plates at the opera house and the hospital.

But stunters live in the back hallways. They hear whispers. They see things they shouldn't. It's better she learns.

"Two years ago, Mr. Davis found this tight rope walker, the Great Blondin. He strung his wire right cross the Gorge. Walked out to the center, had a fry pan and a camp stove strapped to his back. Got to the middle, lit the stove, fried an egg and ate it. Finished his breakfast and kept walking the wire to America."

"Mr. Davis made five hundred dollars on seats in an outdoor pavilion he built special for the show. Made more passing the hat in the crowd. I don't know how much he made on the book, but I tell you, lot of folks bet against the Great Blondin. Lot of folks disappointed when he don't hit the water."

"Now, Mr. Forsyth don't like this. If there's money to be made, well he expects to have a piece. So he bought an old,

old riverboat upriver. Leaky thing, no more than a floating coffin. Docked it on Grass Island and filled it with farm animals. A donkey, cows, sheep, goats, chickens. He bought this old bear, toothless and ratty, from a circus that came to town. You know the kind trained to dance on their hind legs? He sent those dumb animals downriver to the Falls, had a book open on which animal would survive."

"Well you couldn't fit a straw between the people on the shore, both sides, watching that sorry ark. When the animals heard the Falls, they went wild, butting each other. The bear jumped overboard, tried to outswim the current. The chickens, they tried to fly, but they fall. They all fall," I tell her. My mouth is dry. I suck on my teeth a bit.

"Mr. Davis did the sums—he figured Mr. Forsyth paid $50 for the boat and animals. He made $500 passing the hat just in Canada. I don't know about America, don't know about the book on the animals. I thought for sure that bear would make it." I finish but I don't tell her the worst, that animals scream if you scare them enough, that you can hear the screams over the roar of the Falls. She's quiet a full minute.

"Mr. Davis thinks this man, that Mr. Forsyth would steal my barrel?"

I shrug. It makes no sense to say what Mr. Davis thinks, that Mr. Forsyth might try to steal Miss Annie and that she'd be the worse for it.

"Where did the Great Blondin string his wire?" she asks.

"Downriver, cross the center of the Niagara Gorge," I tell her. "He said any closer to the Falls and the mist would have made the wire too slick to stand on."

"Did he carry a pole?" she asks and gestures with her arms, "A long pole that drooped on either side as if there were weights on the ends?" When I nod, she smiles wide. "Well then he was as safe on that wire as he would be walking down the street. That didn't take courage, it took scientific understanding."

She makes no kind of sense. He was a fool, maybe, but a brave fool.

"He was two hundred feet in the air," I tell her, "walking on a wire no thicker than my thumb." But she just shakes her head and holds her arms out like wings.

"The wire is an axis, like the center of a wagon wheel. The danger when you stand on a wire is that you will rotate off the axis, you'll rotate like the outside of a wheel turning. The closer your center of mass is to the wire, the less likely you are to rotate. If you hold a pole while you cross—well the longer the pole, the closer your center is to the wire," she says, and starts talking faster and faster, her arms making the pole and then the wheel. "If the pole is long enough and the ends are heavy enough to hang below the wire—well he's as unlikely to fall from the wire as a man would be hanging from his knees."

She lowers her hands to her sides with a small smile, like she's waiting for applause. She's made up her mind that it was Blondin's pole that saved him and that picture makes her quiet as a hen settled in its nest. She reaches out one hand and places it on the barrel. I've got it standing on a raised stage, ringed with velvet rope twisted like licorice whips. She walks slowly around it with a sigh.

"It looks good, Ab. I'm ready to go," she says and like that she turns like a wheel for the door.

Protection – Annie

The whitewashed walls of the Oxford boarding house are as tired and gray as the face of the landlady. Her every motion speaks of a bone deep weariness. When she hands me the key to my room, it's as if she were lifting an anchor or an anvil, not a slight cast of iron that's only pencil thick.

"It's the first room at the top of the stairs," she says. "There are towels on the bed and a washroom at the end of the landing. You empty your own bed pan."

I nod to Ab before I climb the stairs. I can't see his face through the window, but there's a halo from the gas streetlamp that outlines him in the dark. He's told me he will stand guard all night on the porch.

I am not responsible for myself this evening. I am being watched over while I sleep, like an invalid or a child. It's strange how this makes me feel lighter. I'm like a paper lantern hovering over a flame and I float up the stairs to my room.

I put my hand on the doorknob and it turns. A man pulls me in, clamps his hand down over my scream and I fall.

The Deal – Forsyth

What Davis fails to understand about people is that if he can buy them, anyone can buy them. What he thinks is loyalty is simply a commodity for trade. He thinks this is a safe house, but it's just a run-down boarding house staffed by aging flowers that have turned respectable. It cost me almost nothing to invade.

Paddy pulls the charm into the room and has her scream clamped down before she can even blink.

"Good evening, Mrs. Taylor," I say and I tip my hat. "I'm going to ask Paddy to release you. Please don't scream when he does so, I can assure you, no one here is going to hurt you."

I can see why Davis thinks he's picked a winner. Look at her eyes, flinty in the gaslight, that look isn't panic, it's fury. I nod and Paddy lets her go.

"You must be Mr. Forsyth," she says when she can speak.

"At your service."

"No, I don't believe you are. If you're here to sabotage my barrel, you should know, it's been secured by Mr. Davis," she says.

"Davis has offered you his protection, yet here I am. Aren't you just a little worried that his plans to help you make money from your fall will be equally well executed?" I gesture for her to take a seat on the bed. Being a gentleman, I've taken the chair. She doesn't move. "You're a businesswoman, you should hear what the competition has to offer," I tell her.

"You're not the competition, you're an opportunist. I've heard about the animals you killed just to have a show at the Falls," she says.

"So many ladies object to the drowning of those cows. Yet those same ladies would never turn away from a well done steak," it almost makes me laugh. "Still, the death of an animal is a small thing next to the death of a woman. Or hasn't your bodyguard told you about how Davis paid a New York actress to die in the rapids below the Falls?"

Ah, now that got her attention. I've spent too many hours at the felt not to know a tell. It's not a twitch, not exactly, more of a flutter at her throat. I lean forward.

"Don't tell me you haven't heard of Maude Willard?"

She takes a step back and hits the wall that is Paddy. Well then, she doesn't know about Maude. She steps to the side and sits on the edge of the bed.

"It's true, Davis financed her suicide. Niagara's rapids had already been surfed by one of my daredevils, Carlysle Graham. Fine fellow, local boy. He made me good money. So Davis got a girl to repeat the stunt. Pretty little thing, an actress he found in New York City. Davis convinced her that if she shot the rapids, she'd move from the chorus line to center stage."

"And just to sweeten things for the press, Davis bought her a poodle, a little white ball of fluff with a blue ribbon around its neck, the color chosen to match Maude's bathing costume. You should have seen her hold that little dog up to her cheek, cooing and smiling for the cameras. There were pictures of her in the paper, sitting in the bottom of the barrel, the dog cradled like a baby in her arms."

"They sealed her in and they let her go in the Niagara basin. Tipped her from the Maid of the Mist. That's slow water, but when the Gorge walls narrow, the water runs white. Soon, she was cresting hills of foam, soaring into the air like a popcorn kernel."

I look at the charm. She doesn't realize it, but she's panting just a little bit, her heart must be racing.

"I don't know what Davis told her to get her into the barrel. I doubt he told her the truth, that there's no way to predict the path of a barrel loose in the river. That if they didn't catch her from the shore at Grisham she'd hit the Niagara whirlpool."

"Whirlpool?" she asks and presses her hand to her chest. Well then, I've got her.

"You haven't done your homework, Mrs. Taylor. Downriver, below the rapids, the walls of the Niagara Gorge cut into the river and send it back against itself. Ask water moving that fast to make a right turn and it forms a whirlpool. I've been told by those who've crossed in hot air balloons that the view down into the water is terrifying, like staring into the mouth of Achyllis."

"What happened to her?" she asks.

"Maude circled in the whirlpool for six hours before she drifted to the outer edge and John Stilwell could fish her out with a long hook. I don't have to tell you, Mrs. Taylor, a barrel doesn't have six hours of air."

"But Mr. Davis wasn't worried. He'd taken the precaution of drilling a breathing hole for her. He sealed it with a cork."

"But when Stilwell finally pulled the barrel in and took an axe to the lid, Maude Willard was dead. The poodle had jammed its nose in the breathing hole and smothered its mistress. Davis never figured Maude Willard would be suffocated by the dog."

"That's enough," she says.

"Davis made a good profit off of Maude's death. A pretty corpse is money in the bank," I tell her. She stands, righteously indignant, but I can tell she's leaning heavy on the headboard.

"I have no intention of being a pretty corpse, Mr. Forsyth," she says but her voice is weak.

"Then don't go over the Falls, Mrs. Taylor," I say with a smile. The deal is closing and Davis is losing.

The door smashes open. It's the big Black. He fills the doorframe. Paddy rushes him and they crash into the hallway. I need one second to close the deal and I reach for the door.

The bitch catches me on the back of the head. She smacks me with the china bedpan and I skid into the hallway. I fumble past Paddy down the stairs.

The deal is dead. Mrs. Taylor has chosen the grave. I'll see she lies in it.

Follies – Maude

She brained him with the bedpan and the spider scurried down the stairs. Paddy went tumbling after and they're gone.

"Everything all right, Mrs. Taylor?" the landlady calls up to them. That's what the old flowers are like, prim.

Miss Annie calls for clean towels and hot water in a basin. Ab's eye is swelling shut and the cut in his eyebrow is pouring out blood. She presses her handkerchief to his head.

"Press down hard," she tells him, "The pressure will staunch the blood. Head wounds always look worse than they are." The handkerchief is filled with blood when the landlady appears with the towels.

"Clotting is about pressure," the charm says and dunks a towel in the basin.

"You a nurse, Miss Annie?" Ab asks.

"No," is all she answers him and then, "I was a teacher."

Well don't that beat all? Miss bottle-red with her ostrich feather and her empty barrel, she's a rule maker. No wonder she didn't cow to Forsyth, I bet she's taken the strap to bigger bullies.

But if she was a teacher, what is she doing here?

For me, it was easy enough. I went to New York to be a star and turned out I was as original as a dressmaker's dummy. There were oceans of us, blonde and blue-eyed, coming off the trains and hoping for the stage.

Don't wonder how Davis got me in that barrel. Truth is, he answered my letter. I'd seen Carlysle Graham in the paper — "Man Survives Most Dangerous White Water in the World! First to Surf Niagara Rapids in a Barrel!" But what left the door open for me was, Graham's Canadian. I could have been the twelfth barrel rider to follow him, but if I was the first American, I'd still make the national press.

And I knew what I was buying. Make the cover of *The New York World* and you get a cameo in the Ziegfeld Follies. That's the legitimate stage—goodbye vaudeville! Good-bye hicks screaming "shows us your pink parts" when I'm singing "Danny Boy."

But Miss Annie—she's too old for the Follies, old as my own Ma. So, what exactly is she buying with this fall?

"I want to meet Stilwell," she says to Ab as she's washing him clean.

"No ma'am," he says, "Mr. Davis won't like it."

"A man who has seen disaster will know how to avoid it," she says. It's teacher talk, and don't Ab squirm like a boy asked his sums.

He caves. They'll visit the riverman.

The Slip – Stilwell

I toss two sticks ahead of me and start counting the seconds as they race each other downstream. There's another splash. Instead of my two racers in the channel there's a third. I look upstream. There's a woman, pretty and small, watching me watch the river.

"You're making a map of the river," she says smiling, "Not its path, but its current." She sees more than most. But so do I, and I can tell, she wants something.

"I'm not on the tour," I tell her and go back to my sticks. Let some Charlie tell her about the save yesterday, the kicking bride in the runaway rowboat. I'm sure they're already singing songs about it on the train platform. They probably rhyme my name with "trip to hell." They should sing about Ledge.

If it weren't for him, there'd be no save. He climbed aboard the Marywell and winched us in. Without him, we'd have twisted at the end of that rope until the current tore us over. When I wouldn't pose with the bride, the papers ran his picture, solemn with the rope in his hands. He tells me that picture will get him a girl.

"You want Ledge Ferrell," I say and go back to the river. I need a slow path, an eddy, a channel. I need an advantage. I bend down for another pair of sticks.

"I understand you tried to save Maude Willard," she says.

No photo was taken of Maude after her stunt, no picture of her body. That blank draws the ghouls. They want to know about her last look of panic. They always offer to pay for it, to hear the story of what I saw when I smashed the barrel's lid in. But they can't buy her misery from me. I'll never tell them that Maude's fingernails were broken and bloodied from scraping at the barrel walls. I'll take that to my grave.

"I don't talk to the press," I tell her and move downstream.

"I'm not the press," she says and follows me.

A shadow passes on the ground. I look past her, up the hill. Ab Thomas watches her. He watches me watch her.

"You're not on honeymoon either," I say and I toss another stick in the river. There, where the blue runs three shades lighter, there may be shallows.

"My name is Annie Taylor and I'm here on a scientific expedition." That's just how she puts it, a scientific expedition, as she offers me her hand. I take it, and it's small in mine, like a child's almost.

"What are you looking for?" she asks me and I realize I'm still holding her hand. I drop it.

"A channel where the river runs slower. It'd make it easier to save jumpers if I could pull them into a channel," she's nodding and I almost believe she understands.

"Why do people throw themselves over the Falls," she asks me and those big gray eyes, I swear they're sad.

"Why are you going to do it?" I ask her. She looks surprised. "Your guide gave you away. Ab Thomas guarded Maude Willard, for all the good it did her."

I turn and keep moving downriver.

"I need your help," she says.

"I don't help people go over the Falls, I pull them out," I tell her. I watch her pick her way across the spongy ground along the riverbank. The funny thing is, she's cautious, careful not to slip and fall.

"I have the perfect barrel. I put everything I know about physical science into the design. I can survive the weight of the water and the impact of the fall. I could survive a stampede of elephants if I had to," she says. "Maude Willard was trapped for six hours in the whirlpool but my barrel has only one hour of air. I need your help. I need to know how to avoid the whirlpool," she says and she waits.

"Last year I saved four people upriver—two hydro workers, a fisherman, a pleasure boater. I saved four and the river took forty seven," I tell her.

"I'll take those odds," she replies, "I have to."

Have to, no one has to. I lean forward and catch myself before I tell her what happens to those who have to fall. There are two Niagaras, one here, one across the river in New York, and both cities have an open bounty on the dead. They pay five dollars a corpse to keep the drowned from bobbing up and fretting the guests. The deaths of the sad and the foolish keep the local tramps in hard liquor and old flowers.

"Please," she says and puts her hand on my arm.

There's a moment before you slip when your body knows what it will feel like to hit the ground, so that the crash when it happens feels like memory. I should have looked away from her light eyes.

"Have you ever been to Table Rock to see the water foam as it comes over the Falls?" I ask her and she shakes her head. "You haven't walked behind them, but you're willing to go over them?"

"I have to go over them," she says again. I have to.

"Then you have to come with me on a tour—Table Rock, The Cave of the Winds, The Daredevil's Cemetery. If you still want to go over after you've seen them all, then I'll tell you everything I know about the river," I say and she brightens. She doesn't know what she'll be seeing. She's wrong to hope.

"It's a deal, Mr. Stilwell," she says and she holds out her hand to me. This time I make sure to shake her hand quick and drop it right away.

"When do we begin," she asks.

"Now."

16 Changing – Annie

Once we're inside the wooden barracks built over the entrance to Table Rock, a guide separates me from Ab and Stilwell. All the men file off to the right, the women, so many young brides, to the left. We're to change before our descent.

Inside the women's changing room, the mulatta working the counter hands me a pair of overalls and a shirt.

"Miss, you've made a mistake," I say and I try to hand them back.

"No mistake," she barks and slides them back over the counter, "Everybody in pants. That's oilskin, keep you dry. Next!"

"But these are men's clothes," I tell her.

"Everybody in pants. Keep you dry. Keep you safe. Next!" she barks again and the line pushes me forward, through the curtain of the women's dressing room.

All around me brides are helping each other with their buttons, laughing as they slip from their dresses and petticoats. I watch them pull the pants over their bloomers and adjust the suspenders that keep them from falling down. The pants are made of heavy sailcloth soaked in linseed to make them waterproof. I watch the women cinch straps at the bottom of each trouser leg to pull them tight against their calves. I have never worn pants in my life, and now I am expected to appear in public dressed like some kind of buccaneer.

I clutch the bundle of clothes to my chest, uncertain where to stand in this flurry of women and clothes. In addition to the pants, there's a sort of trench coat with a separate hood.

The brides put them on, tie the hoods under their chins, and become as shapeless as snowmen, indistinguishable from one another by anything but their boots. They kick their legs and squeal at the novelty.

Well then, this is what I must do if I am to fall. I sit down and remove my cuffs. As I undo my shirtwaist I hear my name called.

I turn and the bride from the train, Cecilia, throws herself into my arms.

17 Lean – Cecilia

"Miss Annie! Oh, Miss Annie!" I keep repeating her name as I grab onto her arm. What a relief to see Miss Annie in this horrible place! All these women, they actually seem happy to be putting on pants! Pants! Men's clothes! There's something wrong with them, there must be, why else would they be squealing? And then I saw Miss Annie, straight backed and grim, like any right-thinking woman would be if someone told them to dress like a man or leave.

"Oh Miss Annie, they mean for us to show our ankles. If anyone I knew saw me I would just die," I tell her. She gives me a nudge to sit up and hands me her handkerchief.

"I think pants must be proper in this context, if it is for safety's sake," she tells me. I think she might laugh but then her mouth turns into a straight line and she starts to unbutton her shirtwaist.

"But this is my bicycling costume, I'm already dressed for safety." I reach down to show her the buckles on the hem of my skirt. "I can buckle them around my ankles when I'm cycling, these must be as safe as pants."

"We are in Canada, Cecilia, we must accommodate ourselves to their customs," she says with a sigh.

"But if I'm not careful, someone will see my knees. I don't want this to be how Malcolm sees my knees, they're a little bit knobby," I whisper to her.

"I'm sure your husband's seen your knees," she says.

I don't realize I'm crying until the ladies in pants turn to look at us. I must be making a terrible noise because Miss Annie turns my face to her and gives my chin a squeeze.

"Cecilia, Cecilia," she keeps saying over and over.

"Malcolm didn't want to overtire me after the journey. We came all the way from Saginaw," I say and I must be crying again because Miss Annie keeps saying my name, over and over. I don't tell her how I lay awake all night, wishing Malcolm would at least turn towards me in the bed. I shouldn't even be thinking it. I stop and she wipes my face with her handkerchief, like an auntie would do.

"You just lean into your husband," she says to me and her voice is soft and low. "Lean into him," she says again, "Give him your weight as if otherwise you would fall." I can't help myself, I blush and I nearly get the hiccups.

Miss Annie helps me change into the oilskin. It's funny, I expected she'd wear a whalebone corset like Mama, but she's got regular underclothes on, like a girl.

The men's clothes are strangely slippery on my skin. Miss Annie cinches the pants' cuffs, but barely, and they flap as I walk.

"After the tour, when he helps you into the carriage, tell him you're a little dizzy," she says, "He'll come and sit beside you. When the carriage is moving, put your hand on his knee."

"But, won't he think that's brazen?" I whisper. I don't want the others to hear me. Miss Annie shakes her head.

"It'll help, believe me."

We walk out of the dressing room together. Malcolm rushes up to us.

"I'm sorry, Cecilia, but all the guides are either Black or Irish, we really have no choice," he says.

Black or Irish, what kind of choice is that? No choice at all. Mama would be scandalized!

"Can we use your guide, Miss Annie?" I ask.

"He's right there," she says and points at a big Black coming towards us. Lord, it's like a watching a haystack walk.

"Aren't you afraid of him?" I whisper. I don't want him to hear me.

"I'd be afraid without him," she says. And then she's gone, following his lamp down into darkness.

18   Table Rock – Annie

I follow Ab with Stilwell close behind me. The stairs we tread are wooden and twist through a natural fissure in the rock. The walls are close, we can only move single file. As we descend, the air becomes heavy. Each breath hurts, more water than air. Everything is slick with moisture, where the lantern light hits the walls I see rivulets working their way to the ground and there's a steady dripping from the ceiling onto my hood. I feel my feet start to slide and I throw my arms out to steady myself. Then Stilwell's arms are at my elbows, catching me, keeping me upright.

We emerge from the dark into a strange green light. We're in a wide mouthed cavern that's just to the right of the Falls. White and green foam runs past the mouth of the cave in ropes and ribbons. Endless and writhing like snakes falling from the sky. It makes me dizzy and I turn my face back towards the stairs. I look for Stilwell but I can't find him. Everyone looks the same, all the clothes matching, their backs to me and their faces turned into the mist. My heart is pounding. I step backwards and hit the wall, but no—it's Ab.

"I want to go back," I yell up at him. The roar from the Falls is deafening, but he hears me.

"We can leave, Miss Annie," he leans down, his voice loud and close, "but Mr. Stilwell might say 'deal's off.'"

He's right. This is the test Stilwell has set for me— "You've never walked behind them but you're willing to go over them." He's expecting that this place will frighten me, that I will turn and run.

"I'll never find him," I shout. Ab shakes his head.

"This crowd's on its way to Noah's Ark," he shouts. "Look 'round and you'll find the only other animal that's alone."

It's true. We all came down in threes, each couple led by a guide. Now the guides are lined up against the rear of the cave, only the couples have ventured forward, holding hands or leaning into each other as they pick their way over the slick rock.

I slide one foot forward and then another, weaving my way through the pairs. That pair ahead could be Cecilia, with the hoods I can't see their faces but the woman's pants cuffs are loose and the man is staring at her calves rather than looking at the waterfall. Poor Cecilia, treading that difficult line, always ready to be desired but never appearing to desire.

There, at the mouth of the cave, at the point closest to the Falls, stands a man alone. It must be Stilwell. From here it looks as if he is leaning into the spray. I make my way forward, the sound getting louder as I cross. This must be what it's like to stand inside a furnace, except here the roar isn't flame, it's water.

I touch the man's shoulder and he turns so suddenly that I rock backwards, my heels slipping on the rock. Stilwell grabs me before I fall, his hands at my waist. We're so close to the edge, three feet or maybe four. The rocks beneath my feet tremble and I turn my face away from the water.

It's strange, but the roar is so constant it becomes almost silent, the way you discount the sound of the blood beating in your own ears. Stilwell put his hand on my chin and turns my face back towards the Falls.

From the back of the cavern it had seemed as if the Falls were striking the lip of the cave, wearing the stone away from underneath us, close enough to drown us all. But from where we stand I can see a gap of ten feet separates the rock ledge from the fury of the Falls.

Ab had explained on the way down that we would be fifty feet above the river. I look down, but everything below us is mist. It's like staring into an abyss.

Stilwell lets go of my chin and takes my hand. He turns it palm up and reaches it forward, as if I could catch the water. He is shouting something but I can't understand him. He points and I look up.

Above us, foam falls like snow cascading off a roof in January. Close enough to strike, but missing us again and again. Here comes the endless avalanche and we are safe from its destruction. I laugh and lean further out, as if I were taunting the water—come and get me! And maybe I lean too far because Stilwell pulls me back, pulls me tight against him. I am still laughing when his mouth covers mine.

Then he turns me back towards the cave and the crowd. In the sudden darkness I am snow-blind. He kissed me. There at the edge and now his hand is at my back. He propels me forward and away from him, back into darkness.

19 The Pull – Stilwell

Undressing a woman is an easy matter. But to dress one, to get them back into those layers of ruffles and ties, that's a project of delay. Ab and I wait across from the dressing room with the other guides and the grooms. Every man of us smokes away the time.

We hear the women before we see them. They sound like an argument among starlings. Then the curtains part and they come out, their faces shining, beaming with their accomplishment. You'd think they'd each wrestled an alligator when all they did was parade past the waterfall.

But then, this is what the husband's pay the guides for, to put their women in pants so that they shimmy with the foreignness of their own limbs, send them down into the dark to reach for the Falls, wind them up with the close air and the open water till they're dizzy. Then it's back to their hotels so all those dresses can fall to the floor. It's a trick and a ride, and like a sucker, didn't I fall for it myself?

Here she is. Her face flushed, adjusting her tidy hat and its giant feather. She looks at me but her gaze doesn't climb above the buttons of my shirt. I can't see her eyes. I should apologize, it was a moment of madness. But before I can speak a word against myself, Ab marches her outside the shed. I follow. There's a crowd of reporters.

"Mrs. Taylor! Is it true that you're going over the Falls in the name of suffrage?!" a man shouts at her from behind a camera. "Do you believe women should have the right to vote?"

"Is it true that you're going over in favor of the temperance league?!" another man calls.

The reporters circle her and Ab, and the honeymooners form a second circle around them, each trying to see who the reporters are after, each overlooking the little woman in her ostrich feather hat. Why should it be her?

"Where's the barrel?!" demands the man with the camera.

"At the Table Rock Hotel," Annie says and the photographer collapses his tripod with one hand and takes off running with the apparatus on his shoulder. The reporters shove through the travelers and race for the line of coaches.

I hear a bicycle bell and reach for my wallet. Young Mitchie Nerent pulls forward on two wheels.

"Mr. Davis says to come quick!" he shouts at Annie. "Your agent has arrived. He's called a press conference at the Table Rock Hotel." Then he's gone. I take my hand from my wallet. Mind the boy, it's a reflex.

Ab clears the way through the crowd like Moses through the sea. They all step back and she follows him. I catch her looking for me, even as she's two-stepping to Ab's one. The crowd moves after her, filling in her wake, trying to figure out what makes this little one so special.

I'm pulled after her like a magnet. It's when she's looking from the coach window that I know she sees me. I don't know if there's a softening or a brightening but she tilts her head a bit. It means something, but I don't know what. I'll have to learn it.

My studying lets the man behind me get too close. As the coach pulls away I feel hot breath on my neck.

"Mr. Forsyth would like a word," the stranger says.

Now I know there will be more danger than water.

20 The Flip – Russell

"How dare you?" the widow shouts at me, "I am not the Maid of the Mist—I am not an Indian sacrifice to a pagan god!" She tries to rub the words off of the barrel. God damn it! The paint Davis gave me was too thin. Each letter has already started to run.

"Gentlemen! May I present my employer, the inimitable, formidable, unsinkable, Mrs. Annie Edson Taylor!" I bow to her from my perch on the chair. I gesture for another. The shrew is tiny, but it's the small dogs that bark the loudest.

"That's rich, he promised us a 'maid,'" comes a cackle.

"Old Maid of the Mist!" hoots another.

"Better than a maid, a queen!" I shout as she's lifted onto a chair. Perfect timing. "An adventuress who has single-handedly sailed the Mississippi from its origin in Minnesota to its end in New Orleans. A navigator! Who like Moses was cast upon the Nile and became its ruler. She has come to defeat the mighty Niagara by conquering its most powerful cataract!"

"Are you another Maude Willard, or are you really going over?" comes the question.

"I will go over the Horseshoe Falls in a barrel that I designed—"

"—A barrel designed by divination, from a specter of Charon, the eternal riverman in whose boat we will all one day ride."

"The barrel's based on scientific principles and was constructed by Mr.—"

"—Charon came to her in a dream and said that by this unique design she would survive," I boom. Let her talk like a butterfly, I'll set them straight.

"Damn thing looks like a pint glass," a sketch artist comments. I look over his shoulder, on paper the dimensions of the barrel are clear. It reminds me that I'm thirsty.

"—A pint glass?! Have you no shame?! This barrel is shaped like a lotus flower. The lotus, the only flower to survive on the turbulent waters of the Ganges—" I boom but she's still at it.

"The uneven ends will trap the oxygen around my head."

I can't believe this, she's actually lecturing the rabble!

"I'll spin in the barrel upright, but I won't turn head over heels," she goes on, as if there were a chalkboard behind her.

"When is she going over?" someone shouts. Finally, a good question.

"The test run will be tomorrow and she will fall on Friday. Then it's off to the Pan-American Exposition, Mrs. Taylor will be the star attraction of the closing week!" That gets them scribbling. The Pan Am is big news. We'll ride its tide.

"Friday is my birthday," her tone is off but the line is good.

"Perfect," I hiss at her, "Now you're catching on, more of that, more."

"My friends, she will conquer the Falls on her birthday, a feat no man has managed, though many have tried—"

"—There's one trying tomorrow," comes a voice from the back and I'm cut off. The reporters swing round.

"What do you mean tomorrow? Who's falling tomorrow?" a reporter shouts.

In the doorway of the hotel is a gentleman in a velvet coat leaning on an ivory cane. Standing next to that gent, looking down with a grin, is a milk-fed looking clown, a cowboy hat in his hand.

"Gentlemen, let me introduce Albert Marney," the gent says, "a stallion breaker from West Montana. Tomorrow he means to break the meanest beast of them all! He's going to ride the Niagara!"

Good line, good line, but I'll be damned if that's a bronco rider. The clown kicks at the ground like he can't get humble enough. He's a two-bit vaudevillian or I'll eat my hat.

"Get me ready for the front page, boys," Marney says, "I mean to defeat the Falls," then he raises his Stetson and lets out a ballyhoo.

Like I said, pure pork.

"What time you going over?" comes the call.

"Noon," Marney's still smiling, his hat raised, waiting for the flash.

"He'll have a test run first, at nine," his promoter says. "Allow me to introduce our willing volunteer," and he points with his cane. A big Mick hands the cowboy a white cat. He holds it up with a sly grin. He gets his flash.

"Gentlemen, meet my test pilot, Iagara. You can call her the 'Meow of the Mist'" the cowboy gets the laugh. There's another flash. Damn it! That should be my smoke!

"You're not suggesting that you will send that cat over the Falls in a barrel!" the shrew pushes her way through the reporters. She's got her hands on her hips, school m'arm style.

"Have no fear, Mrs. Taylor," the gent replies, "Unlike yourself, this cat has nine lives." The reporters laugh, even though the line was twisted like a blade. There's something between these two, some kind of history, some kind of danger.

The flashes go off again. If these damned idiots take anymore photos we won't be able to see through the smoke.

Flip it, flip it, there's got to be a way to flip this. That gent thinks he steals my smoke, he steals my thunder, but I can flip it back around before he can wink.

A pint glass is the thing. I'll have a drink and a muddle and I'll figure how to spin Marney around. Make his story the opening act for my own. Falling cowboy, no matter who you've signed with, from now on you're working for me.

21 Sure Thing – Davis

I watch the charm try to clean the "Maid of the Mist" off of the barrel. The paint was thin, so it ran then dried quick. She'll need to sand it off, if it bothers her so.

She went too hard after the Maid of the Mist. When the marks hear that name they think of the boat that takes travelers up to the Falls, they don't think of the legend of that drowned Indian girl. Strange little charm, and this blower she found, look at him sweating.

"Next time, wait for me to answer and follow my lead! You know how to embroider? Well that's what we're going to do from now on," he says leaning over her.

"I don't need to lie," Mrs. Taylor says, all indignation.

"I don't lie. I sell. Don't you understand? Falling over Niagara is nothing without a good story! You can fall only once, you can tell a story a thousand times." Russell starts slapping his fist into his palm and muttering, "Meow of the Mist, Meow of the Mist," fretting over Forsyth and his damned cat.

I admit, Iagara's a good touch, and "Meow of the Mist," that's a good line. But the rub is that cat's stolen from me. What difference is there between her and Maude's dog? They're both small and white. Next thing you know, that cat will be wearing a blue ribbon around its neck.

I tell you, Forsyth is the cheapest kind of thief. And he's boxed me in. What kind of test pilot am I to find that doesn't look like I'm aping him? A damned squirrel?

"What are you going to do about Marney?" I ask as I hand Russell another pint.

"'Battle of the Barrels,'" he says wiping the foam from his upper lip. "I've got them running pictures of both barrels side by side in tomorrow's papers—'Widow and Cowboy Race to Fall.'"

Not bad. But I'd better drop a few fives or Forsyth will have the headlines reading "Cowboy and Widow."

"It's possible Marney won't survive the fall," I tell Russell.

"That'd be the perfect opening act," Russell says and puts his hands in front of him, as if he's framing the picture in his mind. "Marney's barrel in splinters on the front page.

A shot of the rivermen as they solemnly pull his broken body from the water. Arms out, face down, so the buying public has to fill in his final grimace of fear with their own—that would be perfect."

"Are you saying that you plan to cause his death?" the charm asks.

"Well I'm certainly not going to try and save him! If he survives, there goes our meal ticket! If you're not the very first person to survive Niagara Falls, then you'll be the first woman. That's the difference between charging tickets at a dollar or a dime. If you don't want to be the first of the firsts what the hell are you doing this for?"

The charm doesn't respond, just pulls on her gloves in that fierce way women have when they want to reprimand you in silence.

"I'm going to talk with Mr. Marney, that barrel is suicide," she says, then looking at Ab she adds, "I'm going alone."

I give Ab a nod. Now that Forsyth has his own jumper, Mrs. Taylor's safe enough. Let her fume for a while. I give her a courtly bow. I've stolen that move from Forsyth. He's not the only gentleman in town.

"Checking out the competition is very wise," I say as she turns on her heel and leaves.

Well then, the lady is gone and we can all let out our guts and slump our shoulders. I get my own glass.

"What kind of profit do you think you can make off of her," I ask Russell.

"There's the story when she tells it, which in the first week is a dollar a head, second week fifty cents, in a month a dime. Then there's postcards with her picture, splinters from the barrel—we'll sell those like holy relics," he looks at me, "There's the book. What're the odds?"

"So many women faint when they see the Falls," I tell him, "It's thirty to one that she'll even go over."

"She seems the sort to try it," Russell says and looks down into his empty glass. He's getting pink.

"It's a sure thing," I gesture for Ab to join us. "Meet our insurance. Ab will make sure she goes over."

"Miss Annie went to see Stilwell today. He told her not to go over. He thinks he can save her," that's Ab's grim confession.

"Women can't be saved from their own foolish ideas. No man's ever managed it," I tell him.

"He took her to the edge of Table Rock," Ab adds and my smile is gone. Russell looks worried. He doesn't know the attraction, but he can tell it signifies.

"It's a sure thing," I remind Ab, and he nods and slips away.

I don't have to tell him to keep Stilwell away from Mrs. Taylor until she falls. I don't have to tell him that he's to do whatever's necessary to make that happen. I certainly do not tell him that if Stilwell has to be the next body found in the river, so be it. It better be a sure thing.

22 Iagara – Annie

Forsyth's Pavilion Hotel is very grand, three stories high with white Doric columns and a bank of plate glass windows facing the street. In the largest front window, positioned on a plinth, is Marney's barrel. On top of the barrel rests a red velvet cushion, and sitting on the cushion is Iagara, washing her paws.

It's a scene for a picture postcard. I'm sure it is already a picture postcard being hawked somewhere in town. But from every angle, it has to be a joke.

This barrel will kill him. The top and bottom are equally proportioned, there's no difference between this barrel and anything you'd see in the local feed store. Put Marney in there and the barrel won't remain upright in the water. In the first second, it will flip onto its side, spinning him from his stomach to his back. He won't fall so much as he'll roll over the Falls. When he lands he'll either puncture his lungs with his own ribs, or fall on his back and shatter his spine.

"It's suicide." I only realize I've spoken aloud when Stilwell answers me.

"I agree," he says as he steps into the pool of light on the Pavilion's front porch.

"The dimensions are all wrong," I run my gloved fingertip against the glass, tracing the barrel's shape. "The way Marney will spin in the water—he'll break his back."

"I told him just that," Stilwell says and steps closer. I can tell from his tone that the cowboy didn't listen. Maybe Marney assumed it was a trick, a way to scare him into quitting. Why should he believe Stilwell, or me for that matter? After all, Forsyth's made this a race. Now I'm just the competition.

I mean to turn towards the door of the hotel, but instead I find myself turning so that I look up into Stilwell's face. I try to turn again, but my feet won't move, instead, I lean slightly towards him.

All those years in the West, teaching in the high plains and desert, I felt myself drying up, becoming brittle. But the mists of Niagara have soaked through me and I can feel I'm starting to bend, like a branch still green at the wick. I'm relieved and disappointed when Stilwell takes a step back.

"Russell has the reporters drinking at the Table Rock Hotel on his tab. The rate they're going, hangovers will keep them from Iagara's test run at 9. No press, no fall for Iagara. Forsyth won't waste the effort. Wouldn't be a point without the cameras," he takes another step backwards, his hands in his pockets like a schoolboy. "Meet me at the Rainbow Bridge at 8," he says and steps down from the porch and into the shadows.

"Where are we going?" I ask, and his voice comes back to me from darkness.

"Tour's not over," he says and I want to follow him, out into the night.

"You're a fool, you're a fool," I whisper to myself. I can't moon over the only man in Niagara determined to keep me from falling.

I turn back to look at the barrel. I will leave Marney a note and a diagram explaining the barrel's flaws. Let him mind it or throw it away, but let him choose.

I turn back to the window and watch Iagara on her pillow. She looks pensive, as if she can see me watching her. But I know she's staring at her own reflection, puzzling over another white kitten on another red cushion atop another pedestal of folly.

23 Rivals – Stilwell

A man that big has no cause to be quiet, but I don't hear Ab behind me till he swings me round and socks me in the gut.

"I've a message from Mr. Davis. Miss Annie's going over the Falls, don't try to stop her," he says, like he's telling me the time. I'm on my knees gasping.

"It's suicide," becomes five words when I can finally speak.

He kicks me in the ribs and I'm on my face in the dirt.

"Mr. Davis don't like the word 'suicide.' Keep saying it and Miss Annie might start to think her plan is dangerous," Ab says as he crouches down next to me.

I can barely breathe so I don't get the chance to answer, or to warn him. Ab nearly crushes me when he falls.

I look up at Forsyth and three of his hackmen, armed with blackjacks. They'll need them to bring Ab down. They must have caught him on the back of the neck. And that next one, must be a boot to the back, the way Ab is holding his kidneys.

"Gentlemen, I'd like your attention," Forsyth says as he lights a cigar. "We've had fifteen attempts over the Falls since I arrived in Niagara and each one has pulled in a dollar a head."

"Now here comes Mrs. Taylor and her barrel. She's no bluff. Her barrel is scientific. If she survives, my dollar a head disaster becomes a dime a head success. Let me make it clear. The people want tragedy. Nobody went to the Coliseum to see the Christians eat the tigers."

He's right. There's an appetite in the crowds for it. Look at the Great Blondin. After he crossed that first time, no one would pay to see him walk that wire straight. He had to go out on the wire to cook an egg, or carry a hotel maid on his back, or shave with water he pulled up to the wire from the river. Each stunt was unbelievable, but none brought in the money of the first crossing. And now, here's Annie, ready to put a dent in Forsyth's wallet. One thing doesn't hold. Forsyth has his own barrel rider. Why does he care so much about Annie?

"What about your man, Marney?" I ask, "What if he defeats the Falls?"

"People want tragedy," Forsyth repeats himself slowly, each word falls like a coin dropping into a slot.

I shoot forward. Ab is faster, his arms are longer, he's got his man flat on the ground by the time I strike mine at the knees.

It's two on two, Paddy's job being to cover Forsyth's back. Right now he's covering him as they take off down the alley. If you can't fight, you learn to run.

I catch myself laughing as I strike Forsyth's man in the gut. I'm paid to fight the river and I'm nearly always outmatched. But here's a rival that can tire. Here's a beast that can be beaten. Here's a man that can give up. I hit him and hit him and hit him.

Ab pulls me off and the hackman slips down the wall. There's still life in him, but no fight left. The alley is quiet except for the groans. I look around. Forsyth is long gone. I let my tongue count my teeth.

"What are you going to do about Forsyth?" I ask Ab.

"I'll keep Miss Annie safe," he says smiling. His right eye looks puffy. I think the morning will find him a blacker shade of brown as the bruises appear.

"I can't let her go," I tell him.

"Then I can't let you go," Ab says.

A man can think his head is hard, but it takes one hit to make him know it's made of glass.

24 Suspended – Annie

I don't dream of the gun, I dream of the blade. I wake gasping and reach for my thigh. I can feel where the point of the knife left a line of blood down my leg. I'm woken by the sound of my dress tearing away. I wake to know I'm as good as dead.

I don't know the hour, just that it's early. There is nothing to be gained by trying to fall back asleep. Once the dream comes, the bed is poisoned. I might as well head for the bridge. As Stilwell said, the tour's not over.

Outside the air is crisp and cold, good apple picking weather. It's been years since I've seen this kind of fall, years of prairie grass and tumbleweeds that never change their colors. Try explaining to children that know only spiky yucca bushes how a tree's leaves can turn a red so bright it hurts your eyes. Sometime even I started to think what I was teaching was a lie, or at the very least, a fairytale—in winter, the trees leak sugar and cold lace falls from the sky.

I hear a bicycle bell. The boy who advertises bicycles comes close and circles me. It's too early for his bell, but he has it trilling. I understand the principles of momentum that keep him upright on two wheels, but I have never learned to ride. I wave him away.

I passed over the Rainbow Bridge to arrive at Niagara. But from the train you have no sense of the bridge, you can see nothing of what holds you aloft. If you look West, you see a billboard for Coca-Cola strung on wires across the river. If you look East, you see a column of mist rising into the air like a geyser.

From the riverbank, I give the bridge my full attention. The Rainbow Bridge is the longest suspension bridge in the world, strung on wires across the river. It has to be, the water moves too fast to sink piling and the ice floes in winter would easily destroy them. In addition to the longest, it is also double layered. The train runs on tracks across the lower level. Above, carriages and pedestrians get the finer view. I stand and watch as a freight chugs across the tracks. In Niagara, even the simplest transportation must look like a dare.

I stand at the entrance of the bridge and look down its length. The bridge sways and trembles, either from the rumble of the Falls or the train passing beneath me. As I clutch the railing with white knuckles a coach pulls alongside me and the door swings open.

25 Steps – Stilwell

I open the carriage door for her. She peers into the darkness. I hang back, there's no need to scare her. There's a look on her face I can't place, what was she doing leaning over the rail?

"Get in," I say and reach out my hand to help her. Her eyes widen, and like that, it's snuffed out, the look I can't place, gone and replaced by concern.

She takes my hand and I help her inside. She settles beside me.

I try to release her hand but she holds me tight, then takes her other hand and pushes up my sleeve an inch. The rope burns are ugly.

"Are you going to tell me why you were brawling?" she asks.

I strike the roof of the carriage twice and the hack pulls forward with a lurch. She's thrown into me and for a moment she stays, her head on my shoulder. Then she pushes back, straightens herself and rights her hat.

"No guide this morning?" I ask. "I guess Russell and the reporters aren't the only ones sleeping in."

"Did you fight Ab? Did you hurt him?" she asks. I laugh.

"A man that big? I hit the ground and stayed there. Ab ties a good knot, but there isn't a hack driver in the world who can tie a knot a riverman can't undo backwards and blindfolded," I laugh again. It hurts a little less.

She almost smiles, then stops herself and opens her bag, all business. She takes out a small jar. When she opens it, the smell of rosemary fills the carriage. She removes her gloves and gently rubs the salve first onto my left wrist, then onto the right. Heat from the salve, from her fingers, goes deep into my skin. While she works, she talks softly, like she's talking only to herself, as if I weren't here beneath her hands.

"I thought falling would be easy—just a science problem to solve—the perfect experiment, the perfect barrel. But there's so many people involved—Davis, Forsyth, Russell, Marney, you…"

She finishes her doctoring and returns the jar to her bag. I strike the carriage roof again and we slow to a stop. I open the door.

"Look upriver," I tell her. "You see those smaller falls?" From here they look like wide steps, as if a giant had started building a staircase.

"The little dips? They look about five feet tall," she says, one hand shading her eyes.

"That's the distance playing tricks. Those are twenty-foot drops. You won't fall just once. If you go over, you'll crash three times, each fall worse than the last." She only nods and we're silent, watching the river racing towards the bridge.

"Will it be you?" she asks, "At the end, opening the barrel?"

I close the door again and knock on the carriage roof. We roll forward and I wait to catch her when the jolt throws her towards me. But this time she braces herself, ready for the move. She's learning.

26 Rope – Bicycle Boy

When I find Ab to tell him the widow is awake, he's standing on top of a stall door in Mr. Davis's barn. This time of morning, it's cold and the horses' breaths puff up in clouds.

Ab's strung a fat rope across the aisle between the stalls. I watch him toe the rope with his boot. It's taut as a fiddle string. I stand still as I can, he can't be thinking of walking it.

He picks up a pole. Not a pole rightly, but six or seven broomsticks he's bound end to end with twine. He lays this thingum flat across his palms and it droops down like a branch of weeping willow.

He kicks off his boots. I see his socks are gray and darned at the toe with red thread. He presses down with just that one foot on the rope. It stays taut. He slides his foot forward and it catches. Wool will do that.

He strips the socks and tosses them to the straw. Then he slides a bare yellow sole out onto the rope.

I don't think to speak in that silence. There's just the chuff of the horses breathing and chewing on hay.

And he's out! Out on the rope in the air. Just kind of crouched, one foot in front of the other, the pole in his hands jogging left and right.

I know he's only five feet up in the air. I've jumped from a stall door before, there's no fear in that falling. Still, I can't breathe. I can only wait for him to walk into air.

27 Walk – Ab

She said it didn't take courage to cross over the Gorge. That science saved the Great Blondin, as if the pole and the wire did all the work, as if the man was just along for the ride. She said that and maybe she needs to think it, but she's wrong.

Five feet in the air, nothing below me but straw and tamped ground, still my stomach jumps to my throat when I slide my right foot out. My mouth tastes of sick and of metal. My head is shouting "No!" and I shout right back at myself "Now!"

I don't move. Every muscle's locked. Don't tell me it didn't take courage for the Great Blondin to cross. It takes everything I have to push one foot out onto the wire.

There's a feel to it, tension coming up through my foot. I've seen carnival riders stand on the back of a cantering horse. The wire's like that, a living thing.

I grip the pole hard. Reins on a wagon, I tell myself, it's just reins on a wagon. My heart races. Now!

Out! Crouched. So low you can't call it standing. Muscles shaking, like they forgot how to cling to my bones. I can't move. To move is to fall.

"Stand up!" I tell myself. "Stand up!" Slowly, slowly, my legs straighten. I'm up. I'm on the wire. I'm standing. And now?

I think of the Great Blondin. How his back leg swung down, just below the wire, then up to land in front of him. It's not a walk, it's a dance. The weight always on one foot. Come on, now, even walking down the street's about standing on one leg at a time. This is no different, no different at all. I press down my right foot. Drop the back leg. Lift it up. And—still standing!

That's a step! That's one step. I walked on a wire. Even if I fall now, for a spell, I walked on a wire.

My heart's racing. Sweat runs down my face. I take another step. Press down with the front foot. Drop the back foot and lift it up. Still standing!

She was wrong about the Great Blondin, but she was right about the pole and the wire. With every step I take I'm more sure of it, of her, of me.

And then something flows through me on the wire, something right near joy. It's the feeling that I will never fall, never again.

28 The Cave – Annie

The wood of the stairwell creaks under my feet as if my weight could make it crack. I step back.

"These steps are too old, they're not safe," I tell Stilwell.

"They're new, just built in the spring. Every year, ice creeps up the Gorge walls and tears the stairs apart, then the city builds them again," he tells me.

He pulls up the hood of his oilskin. We're not quite a matched set, the rented oilskin slickers reach his knees and my ankles. I step forward and the wood groans.

The stairs run down the side of the Bridal Veil. The spray is constant and my face feels slapped by cold. It would be impossible to fall here, the Bridal Veil is too narrow. Unlike the Horseshoe Falls with its deep river basin, the

Bridal Veil drops into a pit of granite boulders. Yet, Stilwell says there is something to see here.

We reach a platform, twenty feet down from the rim of the Gorge and just below the lip of the Bridal Veil. My oilskin is hurting my rib. I tug at it and realize the source of the pain. I am pressing against the railing, leaning over as far as I can towards the river's edge. I pull back.

"You feel it, don't you?" Stilwell says. I shake my head. "You feel the Falls pulling you!"

I shake my head again, but this must be what the jumpers feel, a magnetic force drawing them forward. I wonder, do they wake when the water catches them, or are they mesmerized until they drown?

A group of tourists in identical oilskins joins us on the platform. I recognize Cecilia and her husband. I pull the hood of my slicker forward to hide my face.

"Why are you hiding?" he asks. I gesture at him to come closer.

"I don't want anyone to see us," I tell him quietly.

"We're not doing anything wrong," he says. But we are. His lips are a half-inch from my ear. If I turned my head, it would take the slightest motion for us to kiss. The steps creak under his feet as he steps back.

"Come," is all he says, and we continue down.

The next platform is twenty feet above the entrance to the Cave of the Winds. The roar is constant. Stilwell pulls me towards him.

"You won't be able to hear me once we're in the Cave," he says, his lips again my ear, "don't leave my side." He has me by the arm and we make the last descent.

Wind gusts from the mouth of the cave entrance as if a storm were brewing just behind the Veil. Stilwell tries to keep me behind him, to break the wind for me as we move forward but I have to feel it so I step to the side.

The wind whips the hood off my head, fills it like a sail. I rock back on my heels, dragged backwards. Stilwell grabs me and pulls me against him. And it is like this, encircled in his arms, that I enter the cave.

The wind tears at everything, my eyes are streaming and my ears ache from the force of the air, the pounding of the water. The water falls just out of our reach, tearing at the stone beneath us. We slowly move forwards, pressing against the wind, and suddenly, we are being pushed from behind. Pushed out and away, pushed towards the curtain and the light. We are outside. I stay in his arms and we climb slowly up the stairs.

I realize he didn't want me to see anything here. He just wanted me to feel the force of this smaller waterfall. He wants me to multiply it, imagine it forcing me forward, forcing me down, falling on top of me, until there is no more me to crush.

Ab is waiting for us at the kiosk where the oilskins are returned.

"I won't have any more violence, Ab Thomas," I tell him and I hear the tone in my voice, a reprimand for the class bully.

"I'm to bring you to Table Rock Hotel," he says "Russell's got the press rounded up."

"Why? Has Marney had his test run?" Ab shakes his head.

"Mr. Russell's got someone with your barrel and she's carrying a hatchet."

Again, I feel the wind in my face. But this time, it's because I am running as hard as I can for the coach, leaving Stilwell behind.

29 The Bulldog – Davis

That bar is mahogany with zinc and if that bitch puts a scratch on it Russell will feel the hatchet next.

Look at her, Mrs. Carrie Nation, holding that hatchet like it's her handbag. She's got to be six feet if she's an inch. And that crowd with her, I've never seen such a collection of hysterics and ministers, all of them wearing miniature hatchets as lapel pins. A fraternity of destruction and misery, that's what Russell has brought us. Look at the press, just waiting for the wood to splinter.

"'Hatchetations' she calls them," Russell tells me, surveying the crowd. "I saw the damage she did to a bar in Manhattan, it looked like a hurricane hit, nothing but glass and splintered wood left. This crowd," he points at the women in black, "they sing hymns while she flays about. She likes to have music while she works." He tries to laugh but it dies in his throat. I can tell, like every man in this room, he's thirsty.

Carrie Nation is costing me two drinks a head, but the bar is closed for the interview. I had Beade bring the palm fronds from the dining room and bank them against the bar. All that's just window dressing if the spirit moves her. They say the Lord tells her when to strike.

The doors swing open and here's Ab and the charm.

"Keep that woman away from my barrel!" the charm shouts. She's panting and her eyes are frantic, like a mother looking for a lost child. It makes her pink and that'll read well in a picture flash.

Russell scoops Mrs. Taylor up, he's got a speech he wants the charm to make.

"Best way to lay the groundwork for your own tour is to follow in the footsteps of hers," Russell tells her. "Now close your mouth and smile."

And our widow comes face to face with God's bulldog.

"Mrs. Carrie Nation, temperance leader, may I introduce Mrs. Annie Edson Taylor, adventuress," Russell says and gives a bow. I'm surprised we don't hear his head rap the floor, he's sunk so low.

There's three small explosions, photographs being taken. The smoke clears and Carrie Nation looks Mrs. Taylor up and down and gives a "humph." That's her judgment.

And the charm, hands on her hips, doesn't she look Carrie Nation over and ape that same loud "humph." The ministers gasp and I swear the hysterics seem to sway.

Russell's right about one thing, Carrie Nation is the most famous woman in America. People can't get enough of her style of temperance work, discouraging drinking by tearing bars apart with her hatchet. If Russell's right, tomorrow a picture of Carrie Nation and Annie Taylor will appear in every paper in America, every newsboy will be shouting Mrs. Taylor's name.

I put my back against the bar. It'd better be only fur that flies.

30 Hatchet – Annie

I can fall only once, I can tell a story a thousand times.

I repeat and repeat Russell's words in my mind as I'm led to face Carrie Nation. We're to sit in identical chairs on opposite sides of my barrel, as if I've invited her to tea. The audience is filled with the press and Carrie Nation's followers. I pray no one mentions that the barrel looks like a pint glass. I pray she doesn't think to expound on the evils of whiskey casks by cleaving my barrel in half.

Everywhere she goes, Carrie Nation is followed by the press. Everything she says is written down and sold. If half of what they write is true, then she has torn bars apart screaming "Gentlemen, I am here to save your souls!"

If a quarter of what they write is true, then she is God's wolfhound, running at His heels and snarling at what He doesn't like.

If one tenth of what they write is true, then I am right to be afraid.

I look her over. We are the same age, I think. It's well publicized that she's married, though she only appears dressed in widow's weeds. It was the desert that broke me of that habit. Hot days in black crinoline will bleed you of tears.

"Mrs. Taylor, do you join me in disapproving of the unhealthy atmosphere of Niagara Falls?" she asks me.

What does she mean by unhealthy? The danger of falling? The suicides?

"I believe the mist from the Falls is supposed to be excellent for asthmatics and those suffering from pleurisy," I say. She takes my words as a kind of agreement.

"Are you aware that in the City of Niagara Falls, there are three ice cream parlors and two Chinese food restaurants?!" Her entourage murmurs its shock at the ratio.

"And that married couples, who should be beyond such base entertainments, are encouraged to visit these establishments?" This meets with louder murmuring. "I have been made aware that the waltz is being danced in this city, the most profane of dances." The murmur of concern from her entourage is drowned out by snorts of laughter from the press. When she turns to glare at them, the laughter is replaced by hiccups.

"Mrs. Nation, you can't mean that Niagara Falls should remove all of its romantic entertainments? After all, this is the honeymoon capital of the world," I say. There's a mild cheer from the audience.

"The complete lack of propriety I have seen extends to those who are not married. Illegitimate couples holding hands, young men stealing kisses before they are betrothed. You must realize, as I do, that men today kiss anything and everything." She hits the words "kiss" and "anything," and they seem to smash against me.

"I am not in Niagara Falls for romance," I tell her.

"I should hope not," she says firmly.

But Stilwell did kiss me, in the coach, on the stairs, in the Cave of the Winds. I feel my face go hot. Russell appears at Mrs. Nation's elbow.

"I think the reporters would be interested to learn why you requested this interview, Mrs. Nation," he says, and drops back again, pink in the face. Carrie Nation lays her hatchet across her lap and takes my hand.

"I want you to join me in my work, to save the lost from the temptations of alcohol." Her crowd coos at the munificence of her offer.

"I am not a minister," I tell her and gently extract my hand.

"But you are a daredevil, Mrs. Taylor. Men like Albert Marney," she spits his name, "think they can find courage at the bottom of a beer glass. You can show the men of this country that true courage lies within. Show them that the true spirit of adventure is never dulled by alcohol."

She turns my hand over and lays a hatchet pin in my palm. The silver gleams in the gaslight.

"Wear this pin. It will bring you luck," Carrie Nation says and her crowd cheers. She reaches for her hatchet and turns her face to catch the cameras.

I realize the hatchet is her crutch. Without it she'd be on her knees, praying for her husband to stop drinking and no one would listen to her but God. But swing that iron and everyone stops to listen. She swings the hatchet and it lifts her up.

She raises it now for the camera, and the gesture is both her victory and her threat. I reach to put my hand on the barrel. I am blinded by the flash of the cameras. Let them keep shooting. Let them print us with our props.

I can fall only once, I must tell this story a hundred times.

31 The Curtain – Ab

One o'clock and Marney has yet to try his barrel. First Russell kept the press abed with hangovers, then his hatchet lady stole the press another while. A stunter won't fall without press, even if the stunter's just a little white kitten. So we wait.

See Forsyth on the upper deck? Spitting nails to be waiting for a cat. 'Course he's getting a cut of the Maid of the Mist ticket price for this view of Iagara's fall. He'll get a bigger slice later when it's Marney falling. Mr. Davis was right to stay ashore.

Miss Annie keeps fretting the time o' the fall. Mr. Russell hands her his watch. He can't be bothered to call out the time. And there's no use in just looking for the barrel coming over, in the glare of day, no man can stare at the Fall's edge for too long without going blind.

"Almost one," she says and closes the watch.

"They'll be setting off from Grass Island," I tell her.

"Three falls, each worse than the last," she says, but I know she ain't talking to me. Must be a calculation she's done about the littler falls upriver, that staircase of water.

I want to tell her about the rope and the pole, about the crossing I made in the barn. I open my mouth and there's a scream.

Every head jerks up as Iagara's barrel shoots the edge of the Falls and tumbles into foam. The Maid of the Mist seems to list, every man and woman leaning to one side, looking to see the barrel pop to the top of the water. We wait.

Every ripple in the water causes a cry, but it's all false alarms. Mr. Russell leaves us for the deck chairs, pulls up his collar and tilts his hat over his eyes. Miss Annie opens the watch again and counts the time down. Ten minutes. Twenty.

The Maid of the Mist carries a lot of fuel, but a half hour in, we're running low. It takes a lot to fight the current and carry folks right up to the foot of the Falls. The captain turns us back to shore, slowly, and once they're not fixed on the Falls, folks start to wretch. You can only stare at falling water so long before it makes you feel strange.

"With the volume of air, the barrel should have popped to the surface like a balloon," Miss Annie says and this time she is talking to me. "How did it get past us?"

I think of the rope and the pole, how I danced in the air. She was right about that, figured out what I couldn't see though I looked hard enough. But here there's dangers she hasn't cautioned. Mr. Davis won't like it, but I tell her.

"Look at the base of the Falls. You see a dark shadow on the foam, about ten feet up from the rocks?" She nods. "That's the barrel. It didn't get past us," I tell her, "It's stuck in the water curtain."

The water of the Falls has a force that only it can fight, and when the water strikes the rocks in the basin, it jumps back up. The barrel is caught in the water's fight against itself. We watch it spin in the water curtain, but it doesn't finish the fall.

I watch Miss Annie's face, and I can see she's figured it. When she strikes the river, the water will hit her barrel both directions at once. She turns pale. I think she might get sick. She rummages in her bag.

"Ab, do you have a lady friend who would like this pin?" she says and offers me the hatchet she got from God's bulldog. It's a shiny piece, but I tell her no.

"I've a lady friend, Miss Annie, but she wouldn't wear a lie like that. She likes a nip in her coffee come winter." And like that, Miss Annie drops it over the railing. It makes a tiny splash.

"I won't let that woman take credit for my fate," she says. She watches the shadow of the barrel behind the curtain as the Maid pulls away. "That barrel's been stuck thirty minutes," she says, "and I've only got one hour of air."

Russell hears that and hoots.

"Wait till the reporters hear that!" he shouts "They'd love to put a dead cat on the front page!" He's up from his deck chair and off to find a reporter who's not busy retching over the side.

"The water curtain and the whirlpool," she says and I can tell she's worried.

"Maybe a cat don't need as much air as a woman," I tell Miss Annie, "Iagara's hardly more than a kitten—his lungs are real small. Iagara could walk out of that barrel like Jonah from the belly of the whale." Miss Annie's considering it. I can tell.

"I can't do that equation in my head," she says, "I tried and I'm lost. I need time to think."

And maybe she can think her way out of this, and maybe she can't. But either way, she has to fall. It's a sure thing.

Air – Stilwell

If the barrel were mine, I'd smash the lid open with the claw hammer. Forsyth has other ideas.

"Careful, Mr. Marney still has to ride in that barrel!" he shouts at me, loud enough for the reporters to note.

I put a chisel against the iron band at the top of the barrel and start knocking with a wooden mallet. The iron band moves slowly, inching upward with each strike from my hand. It feels like time has stopped. Finally, the band is high enough to release the pressure. I wedge the chisel under the lid and flip it free.

Iagara lies at the bottom, crumpled like wet newspaper. I reach down and scoop her out. She's stiff. She's been dead for hours.

"Mrs. Taylor!" there's a shout and flashes. I look up at the bank. The press has gathered in a circle. Annie must have seen, she must have fallen. I thrust Iagara into the first open hands and tear up the slope.

"Give her air! Give her air!" I shout and push my way through them.

Annie's collapsed against Russell. They're both as pale as church wafers. I lift her up and shout at the magpies, "Air, give her air!" They don't stop cawing, but they take a step back, dodging the mallet I'm swinging at them.

"Mrs. Taylor, are you still going over? Mr. Marney, are you still going over? Mr. Marney! Mrs. Taylor!" They don't know who to pester first, Annie or the dime-store cowboy.

I drop the mallet and carry her to a bench. I lay her down as gently as I can. Her eyelids flutter. She sees me and I can breathe. She closes them again and I feel strangled. I should loosen her buttons and stays, but I don't want the cameras catching her undone.

"Put the cat in her lap! Who's got the cat?" a newsman runs towards us, gesturing for someone to bring him the cat as he plants his tripod in front of us. I scan the ground for something to throw—the mallet, a stone. My hand closes on a rock shard and I pitch it at him, striking one of the tripod's legs. If I hadn't been kneeling, it would have taken out the lens.

The reporter swears at me and calls again for the cat. Another reporter runs forward, Iagara held in front of him like a toy ready to be posed. I reach for another stone but before I can pitch it, I see Ab. He's come up behind the reporter and without a word he reaches down and plucks Iagara from the man's hands with a snap as sudden as a heron diving for a fish.

The reporters shout, but Ab ignores them and slowly walks towards the bench until he's standing next to me. He turns back to face the reporters and their camera. I stand up, and together, we block the reporters' view of Annie.

"All right everyone, drinks on me at the Cataract Hotel," Forsyth calls.

Free drink is all it takes to pull them away, but I can tell by the smoke that they got their shots. They got Iagara and Marney. They got Annie lying helpless in Russell's arms. There were not enough stones to scatter them.

I kneel down next to the bench. I don't remove the long pin that holds Annie's hat. I don't unfasten the pearl button at her throat. I don't press my lips against her cheek to wake her. Ab turns to me, cradling Iagara as if the kitten were still alive.

"Back's broke," Ab says. His hand runs down the cat's back, smoothing Iagara's fur.

"She probably smashed around the inside of that barrel like a pebble in a jar," I say.

"Then Miss Annie will need something to keep her from banging around," Ab says. "I've made tack and bridles, I can make her a harness."

He hands Iagara to me and he gestures with his head for me to go. When Annie wakes, she mustn't see Iagara. This is what I've been paid for. I start to climb the hill, I won't bury Iagara near the water, she deserves a better rest. Ab calls after me.

"Remember the Great Blondin?" he asks.

Who could forget that madman? I was there the day he dared any spectator watching to cross with him, carried on his back. You should have seen the men shrink back from the edge of the Gorge, like a wave receding from the shore.

In the end it was a hotel maid who took the challenge, one of the Irish that are blown here by misfortune. She must have figured she had nothing to lose. She handed her bag to someone for safe keeping, hitched up her skirt like she was crossing a stile, and climbed on the Great Blondin's back. The crowd held its breath, willing them both to fall. But they didn't.

"I thought the Great Blondin was magic, that the things he could do were all impossible," Ab says, "Miss Annie taught me different."

The way he says it, it's a warning, but not from Davis this time. Annie's not an investment for Ab that he needs to protect. Ab believes she can fall, Annie's made him believe.

"Don't worry," I tell him, "if she wants to fall after today, there's nothing the devil could say to stop her."

33 Lost – Maude

When Mrs. Taylor wakes, she runs. Who could blame her? Ab might have stopped her, but he knows when a horse needs to lead. He lets her run, away from the river, away from death. Fast as she runs she can't out pace what she's learned.

She could break her head in the barrel. Break it from the spinning or break if from the fall.

She could smash like an egg on the rocks. There's no steering a barrel. Once you're let into the river, you've nothing but luck to say you'll fall from water to water. Plenty of barrels have drifted in the current, shot the rim of the Falls too close to the riverbank and smashed into the boulders that collect on either side of the Horseshoe.

She could suffocate in the water curtain if the Falls won't let her go.

She could suffocate in the whirlpool if they do.

She could leave herself a hole in the barrel for air and watch it fill with water until she drowns.

But I think what scares her most is that she could kill herself by trying not to die.

The harness Ab's after, that harness will stop the spinning from breaking her, but it won't save her.

Charles Stevens tried it. Slid his arms through metal sleeves nailed to the inside of his barrel. Pinned himself to the wall to save his back and head from breaking in the fall. Maybe it did.

But when he hit the Niagara basin, the weight of his body pulled him down through the bottom of the barrel, even as the air inside kept the barrel afloat. Up floats the barrel, and down Charlie goes, paying those metal sleeves no mind.

It took two days to find the barrel, but they never found Charlie. Except for his arms. They were still in their metal sleeves, pinned neatly to the barrel walls. So that's what they buried, Charlie's arms.

Mrs. Taylor's trying to out think this, but she could die from thinking.

She stops in the Devil's Playground, where boulders lie scattered like chicken feed, each kernel as large as a coach. That one, it's larger than the house I was raised in.

She stops. She lets the blood clear from her ears.

She's lost.

They say folks like us—those that fall and those that jump—we will be saved by electricity. The tunnels they're digging above the Falls on both sides of the river, they're two hundred feet wide, they'll hold electric turbines as big as steamships. They'll run the river through those tunnels to turn the turbines, drain the water before it reaches the Falls, and lights will come on in New York and Ontario.

They'll cut the water going over the Falls by a third, maybe by half. Niagara Falls will go quiet. No more thunder, just a kitchen tap to be turned on and off.

That's what will save us. Water so slow a jumper won't waste his sorrow on it. Falls so thin a daredevil could go over in a metal casket, or a rubber ball, or an open boat, and live to boast they beat Niagara Falls. They'll drain her till she's nothing but foam and still tell the tourists that she rages.

The foolish will think she looks fierce. They will look at the Falls, tamed and toothless, and think they know what it takes to stand in the face of fury. They'll think they know what it takes to follow your own bad idea.

Mrs. Taylor starts to run again. She's gone.

34 Circle – Annie

I don't think. I can't.

If I could climb atop one of these stones, I'm sure I could see where I am. I could see the column of mist that marks the Falls. But these rocks are too high and too round, like marbles scattered by giants, no handholds, no crevices, no way up.

I put my head to the rock. Let it roll over. Let it crush me. Stop my thinking.

Ping.

It's faint, but I hear it.

Ping.

It's a bell. I've heard that sound before, the day I arrived—the boy on the bike!

I could wait for him to find me. That's his job, I'm sure. Ab must use him to watch me. He must be looking for me now.

Ping.

I follow the sound of the bell, out of the stones and up a small rise and to the edge of an Indian settlement. A circle of teepees rings a central fire. Again I hear the bell, straight across. I should go around, circle this circle, but it's getting late. The sun is nearly setting and soon it will be too dark for the boy to find me.

I cross. I try to keep to the shadows. Whatever tribe this is, I hope they will forgive me for trespassing.

"Off with you, off with you! No better than a bleedin' tinker! Stealin' in here without a ticket!" screams a brogue at my back. I turn and an Irish woman is scuttling towards me, dressed in buckskin with her hair in braids.

"Do you think teepees repair themselves? Do you think the tea grows native in Canada?" She starts to clap her hands at me, shooing me as if I'm a chicken that's strayed into her cabbages.

"Get out! Get out!" she shouts. Her calls draw others from the teepees—women, children, a few old men. None of them are Indians. All of them are in buckskin. There are stray turkey feathers in their hair. It's not an Indian village, but an attraction, another Niagara stage. I pick up my skirts and run.

I go out the way others come in, through a makeshift turnstile. The barker is missing or I'd buy the ticket. There are harder ways to make a living, but I wonder, does this show go on when the snow falls?

Ping.

The bicycle boy nearly runs me down. I grab the bike's handlebars and he skids to a stop.

"Let go! Let go!" he says kicking. He tries to pry my hands of the handlebars.

"How would you like Mr. Davis to know that I was nearly killed before he could make any money on me?" I ask him, "You nearly ran me under your wheels and I'm his investment you know."

Mr. Davis's name is like a magic charm. The boy freezes and his eyes widen.

"Please, Miss, please don't tell Mr. Davis. He'll set Burke after me," he pleads. The boy may be a guard, a thief, and a spy, but he's also a frightened child.

"Can you let me have your bicycle pump?" I ask and he looks at me confused, "It's the price of my silence." He brightens and nods. I'm asking for a payoff and that he understands.

"Do you know where Mr. Stilwell lives? The riverman?" I ask him and he nods.

"Take me to him."

On Film – Forsyth

"I've got the cat going in with its tail whipping about and then coming out limp as a dishrag. It's going to be beautiful, I got in real close," Dickinson says.

"I don't need moving pictures," I tell him.

"Look, I don't need much. I just need Marney to pretend to get in the barrel, just for the camera. We get that, stop the camera. I cut that footage into the footage of Iagara's barrel going over. Get me? When people watch the film, they won't know they're watching an empty barrel, they'll think it's the real fall."

Dickinson keeps spooling, dancing between my desk and the kinescope. It looks like an icebox with a pair of binoculars cut into the lid.

I tried one of these films in New York. I paid a nickel to see a woman the size of my thumb dance in her underwear. For a dime I could have crossed the street to see a real woman strip down to her skin.

"I'll need an hour to set up downriver at the basin to get Marney coming out of the barrel," Dickinson is still talking, in love with his own story. "The loop will be live cat, dead cat, live man." He stops before he can complete the thought, so I say it for him.

"Dead man."

"Either way, that's a solid three minutes. Run that through this kinescope and you'll have people lining up to watch," he strokes the wooden cabinet like it's a hound he's trained to sit.

"You imagine that people are going to pay for a train to Niagara, and a hotel in Niagara, and meals in Niagara to stand in my lobby and feed nickels into this machine?" I strike the side of the kinescope with my cane and I hear the gears rattle inside. Dickinson leaps to open the door of the cabinet, checking I haven't dislodged something. He's such a small man, I imagine he could crawl inside to make repairs.

"Niagara is a monster open-mouthed at the end of the world. When ancient sailors marked their maps 'here be monsters,' this is what they feared—an ocean of water falling forever. That's what people pay for—to be terrified by something larger than themselves. To grab onto each other in the face of danger. Not to look into a breadbox through a pair of binoculars!"

Dickinson turns to face me, he's gone pink around the ears.

"Say what you want, Mr. Forysth, say what you want— but people want what's new, it don't have to make sense," Dickinson says. "Today nobody wants to make their night soil in an outhouse. No—they want to make it in a closet just down the hall from the bed they sleep in. It don't make sense, but that's what people want!"

This is Davis's doing. He had one of Edison's men film Maude Willard. How she cooed for their cameras, cuddling that dog against her cheek. When she died, Sheriff Dinan confiscated the film, talking about "propriety" and "respecting the dead." I saw Dinan burn the film. The skeins of it exploded like gunpowder.

"How much?" I ask Dickinson.

"Well, we'll need two men and a boat downriver," he looks down at his fingers, doing his sums.

"No—how much for what you've already filmed?"

"Just the cat? No one's going to pay a nickel to watch a cat die," Dickinson says. He doesn't get it.

"No one's going to watch it," I tell him.

Seventy million Americans at the last census and half of them live a day's journey from Niagara Falls. Shrink Niagara to fit in the kinescope and it will end up playing not just in my lobby, but in Toronto and New York and Boston.

Put Niagara on film and no one will pay to travel here to see it. Better to bury it.

Before Dickinson can answer, Paddy swings the office door open with a bang.

"Marney's bolted!" he shouts. "Went into Smith's for rollin' paper n' slipped out the back."

"Damn it!" Dickinson says.

So, Marney's fled. One look at that kitten and he turned tail and slunk. I should have chosen someone more desperate, more eager to please.

"Leave him," I tell Paddy.

"Without Marney all I've got is the cat!" Dickinson bangs about. Getting the kinescope back on its trolley.

"Never mind, I'll give you a five for the cat," and I reach into my wallet. Better take the film before he sells it to Davis as live cat, dead cat, live woman. That woman.

If Marney's been frightened of falling, then Mrs. Taylor must have been frightened as well. And if she wasn't frightened by the fall, she'll need something new to scare her.

Yes, Mrs. Taylor, here be monsters.

36 Business – Davis

"Two more trains of gawkers are expected by noon," I tell Russell. Beade's almost finished with the grandstands. That's a dollar a head, right there. "What's the news for the scribblers?"

"'Widow Falls Despite Cat's Death,'" Russell said, "By tonight, everyone in New York and Ontario will know that she's still going over. They'll be here to watch her fall."

"Sheriff!" the bartender calls. It sounds like a warm welcome but it's meant as a warning for me. I cut Sheriff Dinan off before he reaches the reporters, I grasp his hand and pull him to my end of the bar.

"Sheriff Dinan, good to see you! To what do we owe this honor?" At "honor" the bartender pours something expensive, quickly. The first class bourbon appears on a tray at my elbow, if I'd said "pleasure" instead, Sheriff Dinan would be drinking off the second shelf. "With my compliments," I say as I offer him the glass.

"I'm not here for that rot. I'm looking for a Frank M. Russell," Dinan says and Russell sneezes. "Seems Mr. Russell has some mad woman convinced to go over the Falls. I'm here to stop it."

"Are you going to stop Albert Marney, too?" I ask. Seems only fair, if I'm to lose out on my investment, Forsyth should also feel the pain.

"Don't have to, Marney's called it off! He's not stupid enough to follow a cat into hell," Dinan says, and I can see him eyeing the glass of whiskey.

"Fantastic! Think of the press—'Mrs. Taylor Dares What Marney Feared!'" Russell slaps the bar top with pleasure.

"I cannot afford to have a crazy woman kill herself—" the sheriff shouts.

"—She's not insane. She's a daredevil. She sailed the Mississippi single handed from its origins—" Russell starts his barking and Dinan pushes him away.

"If she tries to go over, I'll arrest her. Since Maude Willard died with her damn poodle, my wife's been on my back. She goes on and on about the poor widow woman who is throwing herself over the edge and no one lifting a finger to stop her. She acts like I killed the woman's husband and left her a widow."

"The poodle didn't die. I can send it to your wife" I tell him.

"If Mrs. Taylor dies, I'll find Mr. Russell and I'll have both of you tried for accessories to murder," he finishes and puts on his hat.

"What if I had an envelope ready for you this evening?" I ask. It never hurts to ask.

"Are you deaf?!" Dinan explodes, "You've upset my missus! I won't have two minutes of peace till I stop Mrs. Taylor."

"What if Mrs. Taylor goes over and survives?" Russell asks.

"Then I'll have a doctor and a straight jacket waiting for her. I'll see her in Thornhill Asylum before she can shake the river from her hair," and with that he's gone.

I see Russell eyeing the drink and I lift it to my lips. With the first taste I know I was right never to marry, it makes a man do unnatural things, like refuse free liquor and good money.

"What do we do now?" Russell asks.

"We're in the business of Mrs. Taylor falling. We're not in the business of keeping her alive, out of the asylum, or out of the county jail. So we do just that," I tell him. "We see her fall."

37 Quiet – Bicycle Boy

"They say Mr. Stilwell reads the river by looking at the sky. I asked him and he said that's a half cup of truth. He can do it in winter on cloudy days when there's ice on the river. He can tell where the ice is melting by the way the river's reflection streaks the clouds. I don't think he's joking. I think it's true. I think that's how he knows when the ice pack will melt. They pay him for that too, the town does," I tell Mrs. Taylor.

She makes me walk my bike beside her. She says my circling her on the bike makes her dizzy. It's a slow tread to Stilwell's place. Something's gotta go fast, so my mouth is running.

"They say Mr. Stilwell dreams of ice, 'cause he hates when he can't see the water. My Mama says one winter the Falls stopped. Just dried up, no water, nothin'. It near drove Mr. Stilwell mad."

"There's no way to make the Falls freeze," she says quietly.

"It's true. Ice upriver got so thick that when it broke, it jammed up the Niagara River like a giant beaver dam. The river dried to nothing. They say you could walk in the river bed, right to the edge of the Falls and pick up arrow heads and muskets and all manner of ancient things that'd been lost in the French and Indian War."

"And Mr. Stilwell, Mama says, was the one who woke the town to tell them the Falls had run dry. Only he wasn't calling that. He was running through town yelling 'Too quiet, too quiet!' Imagine someone waking you up to tell you it's too quiet. It's like them waking you up to ask if you're asleep."

"He couldn't hear the river, and it woke him," she says, real soft.

"Yes'm, Mama says that's when he moved out of town," I say. "This is it." She looks startled, like she was expecting a house. But long as I've known him, Mr. Stilwell's lived in this cave, upriver of the Falls, looking out towards Grass Island.

We can't knock, seeing as how there's just an oilskin curtain on a clothesline for a door. So I call to him and when he doesn't answer, I just pull the curtain back.

It's dry in there, homey, but small. Just a cot, a table and chair. A little camp stove. There's a rumble all around, not just the sound of the Falls in the air, but a rumble coming up from the ground.

"There's no way to block the sound of the Falls, there's no way to stop it," she says. She has her hands to her ears and her eyes squeezed shut.

"In good weather, he sleeps on his boat," I say. I don't know why, but the place makes Miss Annie's eyes fill. She looks like a prayer card of the sorrowful Madonna, sad and lit up at the edges. But before I pinch myself, I see she's not really glowing, it's a lamp at the cave entrance.

Mr. Stilwell has come home.

38 Stay – Stilwell

I would have told her, but not like this. It's the kind of thing you whisper in the dark, holding each other, both half asleep.

I am no one's idea of home.

I cannot save you.

The river owns me.

I dream of ice.

Stay.

39 Stones – Annie

I don't realize the fantasy I've built until it crashes around my shoulders. Even as I asked the boy for the bicycle pump, so that I can squeeze as much air into my barrel as possible before the launch, even as I was saying it—there was a part of me that wanted a smaller life, a quiet life of keeping home. No, of being kept.

I look down at the ground, as if the remnants of that dream were spread out in the dirt—there's the little cottage, the cozy kitchen, the warm stove burning as the snow falls. The type of dream where there's plenty of coal in the bucket, but when you lift it, the handle never cuts into your hand. A home with no pain and no work, as if all we would need is the pulse between our two bodies.

It's the same dream I had about David. I was a girl then, I could still believe. But now I must see clearly. I lift my head. Stilwell lives in a cave. He's tied to the river. He can never leave it.

"I've come to finish the tour," I say. Stilwell only nods and steps back, out of the cave, holding the oilskin flap up for me.

"Remember our deal," I tell the boy, "Bring the bicycle pump to Ab Thomas." Then I follow Stilwell out into the night.

Even with the lantern before me, I stumble. Stilwell catches my hand, stops my fall. We stay that way a moment. He holds my hand the way you balance china in your palm, the way you hold a baby chick. It can never be more, so I let it be everything. No lamp, no path, only the dark and the feel of his palm against mine. I try to make it enough. With my hand in his, bound inside a tiny circle of light, we walk.

The Daredevil Cemetery is on the other side of town, out of sight of the travelers and the Falls, but even here, if you listen, you can still hear them roar.

We move from stone to stone. Before each he raises the lantern. There are no dates of birth, just the stunters' names, the stunt that killed them, the day of their death. Everything they were has been boiled down to their attempt to go over, or behind, or across the Falls.

"When my baby died, my husband bought three plots side by side. It eased my mind to know we would all be together," I tell Stilwell. It feels strange to speak to him about David. "But after my husband died, I had to sell my plot to stay alive. Some other woman lies beside my baby now."

"I'm sorry," he says and gives my hand a gentle squeeze.

"Show me where," I say. Stilwell leads me to an empty spot on the edge of the cemetery, a section of open grass that is waiting to be filled. On one side of it is the cemetery wall, on the other, a tombstone larger than any of the others.

"Who is that?" I ask. Stilwell holds up the lantern so I can read the inscription, there are no names or dates, it simply reads "Ice Bridge Tragedy."

"No one knows their names," he tells me. "Newlyweds and an unlucky man who tried to save them." He pauses and touches the stone. "They were climbing on the ice bridge when it collapsed. After they died, well …it's a crime to climb on the ice bridge now." He doesn't say that it's a crime to go over Niagara Falls in a barrel, though that's also true.

I want to ask him if he can he really read the river by looking at the sky. I want him to tell me a fairytale where I walk out of the barrel and never come back to this place again. But that's not the deal we've struck.

"What happened to them?" I ask.

But what I mean to ask is—what happened to you?

40 Crossing – Stilwell

"In winter, ice forms on the surface of the river basin below the Falls. But it's not smooth like the surface of a pond. It's jagged from ice floes upriver being thrown over the Falls and freezing where they land. All winter it comes, ice beating onto ice, and nowhere for it to go but up. The ice starts to climb up the sides of the Gorge, up the front of the Falls themselves. I've seen sheets of ice climb thirty feet against the Falls."

"It was an attraction for both Niagaras. They called it an ice bridge because you could cross from Ontario to New York on it. But it's not an easy walk, there's no clear cross. There are hills and walls of ice that have to be scaled. Every year they had a boy's race from the U.S. to Canada, and it could take over an hour for the runners to clear the bank, that's how rugged the hillocks of ice can be."

"And all of it shivers beneath your feet. The ice can be ten feet thick, but still it trembles with the rage of water flowing underneath."

"The city built temporary pubs on the ice so men could have a beer standing on the river. There were carts for roasted chestnuts and coffee. They had paid excursions where they'd lead couples right up to the cataract, closer than you can get on the Maid of the Mist. And at night they built bonfires on the ice. All that weight and heat, and the ice is trembling, the river is moving, but no one minds. And one day, the thaw came early."

"Nobody felt it. There was no change in the temperature of the air, but the water going over the Falls, the water running under people's feet, had gotten warmer. When the thaw comes, it starts first at the shores, cuts the ice bridge off from land. I was there and I didn't know the thaw had come until the ice began to crack along the riverbank."

"When people realized they were no longer on a bridge, but floating on a patch of ice, they started screaming. People panicked, pushed into each other, trying for either shore."

"In the middle of the ice bridge were the newlyweds. They tried to make the American shore, but there was eight feet of icy water between them and the shore, they had no way forward, so they turned back and headed for Canada."

"The ice bridge started to break into floes, and those chunks of ice tear downriver as soon as they're loose. The husband could see this, and he started dragging his wife by her arms. She couldn't run because of her dress and the heels of her boots. She couldn't climb the hills and so he'd drag her around them. They'd disappear and we'd hold our breath on the shore, and they'd come around the other side and there'd be cheering. Like it was just another race."

"And then a man left the riverbank and sprinted for them. I'm sure he thought he and the husband could just carry the bride off the ice. He reached them just as the ice bridge gave way and the ice they were standing on started floating downriver."

"They tried to jump from ice floe to ice floe. The stranger, he crossed to one floating near by. He held out his hand for the bride. And the newlyweds leapt. They made the second floe. And I thought, we all thought, they were going to make it. Even though the river's moving and the ice is melting, I thought, they can do it."

"And the stranger and the man are talking as they start to drift faster and faster downriver. And the bride, she sank to her knees. Maybe she was praying. And the ice floe they were standing on flipped over, threw the three of them into the river, and they disappeared beneath the ice."

"We didn't find their bodies till late Spring. By then, no one could tell the groom from the man who tried to save them. The city buried the three of them together."

I stop. I don't say the awful truth, that this should have been my grave. I should have saved them.

"How many did you rescue that day?" she asks. She is standing just outside the circle of lamplight. It's a gentle question but it catches me in the gut. I can barely breathe.

The men afraid to jump from the ice to the riverbank, I pushed from the ice floe to the shore. There were children, boys that had been in the crossing race. I picked them up and threw them to the shore. There was a woman, I threw her over my shoulder and jumped.

"How many did you rescue?" she asks again. I shake my head.

"I can't help you," I tell her and I watch as something in her closes up and shutters tight.

41 | The Tour – Annie

"I'm sorry, I can't," Stilwell says. And there it is—the crack in the ice that he cannot leap over.

Stilwell doesn't understand, I am already in the water. I am already racing for the edge. If he won't help me, I will still fall. I am already falling.

"Everyday I wake up cold with an ache in my hands…" I tell him as I take off my gloves. I show him how the knuckles have swollen, how my fingers cramp up, although to draw his attention this way makes me tremble.

"I can hardly hold a piece of chalk anymore. I can't ply a needle and thread. What is left for me to do but laundry and lye soap? Working until my hands bleed? Earning just enough to live another miserable day? I can't do that. I won't."

"If I fall, I can live off my story. I can have a warm room and plenty to eat. Russell will see to it."

"I could take care of you," he says. My eyes fill with tears. So, we share the same illusion, that we could be together, that this force that pulls me towards him, that pulls us towards each other, is greater than the pull of the Falls. We're both pretending that he isn't a captive, a dog tethered by a short lease to the river's bank.

"You can't save me, however much I might want you to," I tell him. "I can't live waiting every day for the river to claim you. I'd grow to hate you, we'd grow to hate each other."

He says nothing. Just takes my hand and strokes a finger over my swollen knuckles. That gentle touch is a streak of fire up my arm. I have to go.

I take the lantern and turn to leave. There is nothing to be done. If I fail, it's here I will lie. It will be Stilwell at the end. He will find the barrel and free me. He will lift me gently, like a sleeping child taken from her cradle. He will dig my grave and cover me over.

In the end, it will be him.

Epitaph – Maude

She stops to see me on the way out, to read what's written on my stone.

Maude Willard
Whirlpool Rapids
September 7, 1901

Well, better that then "Maude Willard, Starved," or "Maude Willard, Not Enough Money For Coal."

No, a stone was always waiting for me. At least this way I'm not "Maude Willard, Forgotten."

Annie traces the letters of my name in the gray granite. The chiseling is so fresh it could cut.

"Are you another Maude?" that's the question they all ask her. She doesn't want to be, and fair play, I didn't want to be either.

But there you are, you fall and sometimes you sink.

43 Asylum – Forsyth

"You've come at a difficult time," Benson says. He's the resident alienist, meant to give us the tour of Thornhill, to show us the best that can be offered in patient care and accommodation.

Seated at his desk, his head is mirrored by a wax model of a bald man's head, the skull tattooed with a map of deceit, lust and greed. The "Science of Phrenology" they call it, the bumps on the skull telling what ails the brain inside. As if a man's skull was a book written in Braille, telling the patient reader his every thought. If that were so, I'd have a spy in every hat shop in the city.

Still, this lovely bunkum lends a sheen of respectability to this hole in which we throw the forgotten. It makes it seem scientific.

"Once the sun sets, darkness loosens the strings on the patient's fears. What we spend the day in treatment binding becomes unbound in the night," Benson continues, nearly as waxy in complexion as the Phrenology model.

It was my idea, this trip to the asylum after dark. During the day it's clear that Thornhill is a prison. But at night, isn't everything sinister? Dinan knows that there's a difference between Niagara in the morning and at midnight. Show him Thornhill now and later he'll convince himself that it's a hospital, that the only thing that frightened him was the night. That's what I'll tell him if he balks when we're done with our tour. It was only the night.

We follow Benson down a maze of stone corridors lined with locked wooden doors. At the top of each door is a window set with metal bars, at the bottoms are leather flaps through which food and medicine can be delivered. From each door we pass comes the sound of pain. Dinan walks quicker and closer to me the further we go.

The alienist pulls a ring of keys from his coat pocket.

"We've made remarkable progress with attempted suicides," he says as he fumbles with the lock, "largely through the use of water therapy."

Inside the room, a man in a white nightshirt lies on a table. He strains against leather straps on his wrists and ankles so that he bows up from the table in an arc of pain. Benson gestures at an orderly.

"Continue," he says.

Above the patient, near to the ceiling, a tank of water is suspended. The orderly pulls a chain and the tank tips forward. Water flows down onto the patient's head in a steady stream, as if he lay under the spout of a well pump. The patient screams. I'm sure from the cold, the bright shock of its strike.

The water continues falling. It runs down the sides of the table, down through a drain in the center of the floor. The water falls until the man stops struggling and surrenders. Dinan is standing so close to me, I could take his hand like a child's. The patient lies still. The water drains away.

"Impressive," I say. My voice sounds strange in the room. Thin and unsteady. It must be the effect of the stone.

"I think you will find that we can offer the best care for attempted suicides in the State of New York," Benson says. "And of course, we're uniquely positioned to help, being so close to the Falls," he gestures to the orderly.

"Administer a second dose," he says and then leads us out, locking the door behind us. The orderly and the patient are both prisoners until Benson returns.

"This way," Benson says and we're led deeper down the corridor. He unlocks another door. It's an empty cell, maybe six feet by eight. Nothing to see but a narrow bed outfitted with leather restraints. The sheets are crisp and white.

There's a small window high on one wall. I turn to Dinan, summon up my face of compassion and gesture at the bed.

"Are we agreed?" I ask him.

When he nods, his head hardly moves. His eyes are trained on the small window, at the narrow square of night that can be seen through it.

"Could this room be ready for tomorrow morning?" I ask Benson. The alienist nods.

"The name of the patient?" he asks.

I turn to Sheriff Dinan and wait. He addresses the window and his voice is small.

"Taylor," Dinan says, "Mrs. Annie Edson Taylor."

44 Drawn – Stilwell

This is how it began.

I shared a room in the Redmond boarding house with five other men, but at night, I never heard the sound of them snoring. Everything was drowned by the sound of the Falls, and I slept all night dreaming of water. And then the noise stopped. It woke me with a shock, as if I'd been shot in the leg.

I woke the others. They were angry till I told them to listen. The city was silent. I threw open the window. The wind was ice as it pushed into the room but still we could hear nothing. We raced to lace up our boots and headed for the river.

Outside we were not alone. The silence slowly woke the town and lanterns came around every corner as people started toward the Falls. I was the first one there, racing through the dark towards that gap where the pounding of the water should be. With the lanterns, we could see ten feet in front of us, but there was nothing to see. No water at all.

The Falls had stopped because the river had run dry. It was as if the Lord had been pumping a well handle and had tired of the chore.

People thought it was the end of the world. That the sun wouldn't rise. That we'd been caught in the Rapture of the Apocalypse and would await our doom in darkness.

More and more people came to the riverbank and we built a bonfire so that we wouldn't freeze waiting for the sun. And I thought something wicked was beyond that circle of light. No water, no thunder, no God.

By the time the sun rose that morning, a cable arrived to tell us that an ice jam upriver had damned the Niagara River a full mile away. By then, the crowd on the riverbank had doubled. Ladders started to appear. People climbed down into the mud of the riverbed and started to look around.

They found bayonets and tomahawks in the mud, remnants of the French and Indian War that had drifted downriver. Some people scrambled to the very lip of the Falls to look down into the basin below. I wanted to scream, "it's too quiet," but I was put to work.

A body had been discovered on a ledge below the Falls. A jumper that'd been hidden by the water curtain for Lord knows how long. I had time to be winched down in a bucket, to wrestle the body, a man, into a gunnysack, and carry him back up to be buried. From the bucket I could see the channels carved near the lip of the Falls. I had time to think.

Just before noon there was an alarm from upriver, a cannon fired to let people know the river was free and awake.

People were still climbing back onto the riverbank when a stream of water came gushing down. First a trickle, like a milk can kicked over, and then suddenly a wall of water. It looked like a living thing, like horses galloping, racing each other for the edge.

And something took hold of me, a push to jump in, the idea that I could master them, those horses of water, that I could drive them forward even faster, could lead them over the edge to—what—the sky?

And maybe I might have, if the river weren't faster than my thoughts. The water crested and flowed over. The roar returned, unyielding, unending. Folks wandered back to town. Their miracle was over. I just stood there, shaking.

The river came so close to claiming me that day. And I cannot shake the feeling that the river is patient, it's waiting for me.

The jumpers I go after, I know before I hit the water that the river is ready to claim me. If I fail and the river takes them, I know that is what the river will do to me. That is what it's already done.

The save that brought Annie to me was the bride in the rowboat. But what Annie couldn't see was that even as I raced for the girl, the river pulled at me, demanding I give up, that I go over. I could only fight the river because the girl needed saving.

Standing on the riverbank Annie saw me save the bride. But I know that I was drowning and the girl saved me.

45 The Captain – Ab

There's some men think they don't have to keep their word if they give it to a woman or a child. I never figured Stilwell for one of them.

"The tour's over," is all Miss Annie says when she finds me waiting for her outside the cemetery. Tour's over, but she left it empty handed. Escaping the water curtain, the rapids, the whirlpool, they all still hang over her head, each an axe ready to fall. Whatever Stilwell knows of them, he kept to himself.

Still, there's other ways to keep her on the wire.

We came straight back to the barrel, planted like a flag in the front window of the hotel. Soon as she arrived, she pulled the curtains closed. The crowd outside started knocking on the glass, but she put her back to them. She forgets, they're her paying customers, even if she's just thinking they want to watch. But she doesn't pull the curtains open, and after a while they stop their knocking 'cause there's nothing to see.

She taps the barrel lid and without the last iron ring to hold it in place, it flips up. She grabs the lid in both hands, and carefully places it on the floor beside the barrel. She can't afford to have anything happen to it.

"Did that boy bring you the bicycle pump?" she asks and I nod. "Good. I need you to drill a breathing hole for me." She leans forward to look inside the barrel, placing one hand on the inside wall and one outside, as if feeling the smooth curve for something. A second later she chalks an "X" between the eighth and ninth bands, just above the black "Q" in the "Queen" Russell painted. "I'm not going to bet on one hour of air," she says.

I feel a shiver go down my spine, like a ghost has moved through the room. Maude Willard didn't pick her barrel, Davis chose it for her. He chose the barrel and the costume and the dog. Miss Willard went along for the ride, not even a passenger, just cargo to be shipped downriver. Miss Annie's barrel is little better. Still, she's trying to be a captain, she's trying to make it a boat.

"I made you something," I say and hold out the leather harness. "You slide your arms through, like you're putting on a jacket. It'll pin you to the wall of the barrel. Keep you from banging around." I don't tell her about Iagara, her tiny broken back, but Miss Annie understands just the same. "I can attach it to the inside with short nails so the barrel stays dry."

She nods and takes the harness in her hands, turning it over gently, as careful with it as she was with the barrel's lid.

"This is such fine handiwork," she says, "You could have your own tack shop." She hands it back to me. "Will you attach it for me?" she asks and I nod.

She leans back into the barrel, makes another X with the chalk.

"Here" is all she says, then stands back and lets me get to work.

First I drill the hole and she asks me to tip the barrel so she can try it out. I lay the barrel on its side, then turn my back until she tells me she's inside. I tip her back to standing and look down into the mouth of the barrel. Even without the harness, there's little room for her to move.

"I've got something for you," says a voice. I turn and it's Stilwell standing in the doorway carrying an anvil in his arms. Not the kind you set for horseshoes, but the smaller one, the kind you set for chain links or straightening nails. Miss Annie stands up and the barrel circles her like a second skirt. She watches Stilwell lower the anvil to the rug.

"Are you planning to throw me in the river with that tied around my neck?" she asks. Stilwell is as grim as the reaper. He noses the anvil with his boot.

"It's not for your neck," he says, "it's for your feet."

And I don't know why, but she's laughing.

46 Ballast – Annie

First I press my mouth to the breathing hole, to make sure I can reach it with just a turn of my head. It works and I tilt my head to look out through the small hole.

Stilwell. I can only see the tanned backs of his hands but I know him in an instant.

I struggle to stand and Ab reaches forward to steady the barrel. Stilwell carries a black anvil. I want him to lift me from the barrel, peel it off me like a layer of clothes. I want to grab him and swing him about.

"I've thought of it from every angle," Stilwell says, "In order to escape the Falls, you have to be heavy enough to fall through them. If you're too light you'll get trapped behind or within the water curtain. Iagara was too light. You need ballast," he says and puts the anvil down.

Stilwell steps towards me, puts his hands at my waist and lifts me from the barrel. His face is grim, as if I'm just cargo to be carried to shore. He puts me down and steps back.

"Come, I'll show you."

We follow Stilwell into the lobby, to the Horseshoe fountain.

"Wait here," Stilwell says and disappears behind the bar. When he comes back, he's got a cork and a corkscrew in his hands.

"This cork is you," he says and drops the cork into the top of the fountain. The cork races forward, shoots over the lip of the Falls and disappears into the water. We wait, but it doesn't flow out into the basin that's cluttered with pennies.

"There," Stilwell says and points to where the cork is spinning behind the water curtain.

"It's trapped," I say to Stilwell and watching it makes me short of breath, as if there was a hand at my throat choking me.

"If you're too light in the barrel, you'll spin in the water curtain, caught between the water falling and the water pushing up. You'll never reach the basin or the river. But if you're heavy in the water, if the barrel is so low that you're barely keeping afloat, you might have a chance," he says.

Stilwell grabs the cork from the fountain and shakes the water onto the carpet. He twists the cork onto the corkscrew, till it's run completely through. He drops it into the top of the fountain, into the well of water above the Falls.

Again, the water pushes the cork forward, but only the tip is visible in the water. It moves slowly, dragging the corkscrew along the bottom of the fountain, inching towards the edge of the Falls. It tips over, falls down through the curtain, and bobs up, barely above the water of the basin.

"You've got to be heavy enough to fall, not just down, but through," Stilwell says and takes the corkscrew and cork from the water. He tries it again, back into the basin at the top of the fountain. Again, it falls down and through, floating above the copper pennies.

But how heavy is too heavy? Too much weight and I'll fall through, straight to the bottom of the river. The basin beneath the Falls is said to be twice as deep as the Falls are high.

"You can't put an anvil inside the barrel with Miss Annie. It'll bounce around, break every bone she has," Ab says.

"You'll have to fasten it beneath the barrel, like a boat dragging an anchor," Stilwell says.

"We'd have to drill holes in the bottom of the barrel to secure it, even if Ab caulks the holes over, it won't be waterproof any longer. I'll take on water," I say.

Take on water and I take on weight. The more water in the barrel, the less room for air. Stilwell's plan could save me from suffocating in the water curtain just to drown me inside my own barrel.

"The anvil's fifty pounds, the barrel's oak, probably another 50. With you in it, you'll still float, but you'll be low in the water. The weight should carry you through the Falls and into the river basin."

"Let's say I do this, and with the anvil I clear the water curtain. How do I avoid the whirlpool?" I ask him.

"The river has its own mind. It'll take you where it wants. But once you clear the Falls, I'll try like hell to catch you. If I can't fish you out, we'll hit the rapids together," he says.

That's the best that he can offer me, that we will both go down together.

"Ab, can you make this work?" I ask.

"Like shoeing a horse," he says and I nod.

"Then let's do it. Let's weigh it down," and I scoop the cork from the fountain's basin, the tiny ship that survived, the lucky charm.

"I'll need another cork for the breathing hole," I tell Ab. He nods and heads back to the bar. Stilwell and I are left alone by the fountain.

We will both go down together.

47 Jonah – Stilwell

It is almost midnight, the last minute of her last day. I don't want to think it, but there it is. Her time is running down.

I watch her lean against the railing of the Marywell, watch her as she watches the river's current. She has the lantern in one hand. In the circle of its light the river looks slow and calm. It's a lie.

"Ab's been quoting the book of Jonah to me," she says. "'Take me up and cast me into the sea, so shall the sea become calm for you.' Those are Jonah's last words before the sailors toss him over the side."

Wasn't that why the Indians sent that girl downriver, as a sacrifice to their god of the Falls? Did it work?

"Years ago I saw a magic lantern show of the Holy Land," I tell her, "and in every picture was the desert. Nothing to look at but sand but all the Bible talks about is water." I stand beside her at the rail.

I sometimes wonder if the Maid of the Mist was really a human sacrifice to the river god. Sometimes I think she stole the canoe herself, determined to disappear into the world on the opposite bank. Maybe she just got caught in the current. Maybe she didn't even mind. Maybe she was just another jumper dying to fall.

"I hear music," Annie says.

"It's from the Pavilion upriver. Sound travels easy over water. Careful what you say or folks might hear of your secret plan to go over the Falls tomorrow," it's a weak joke, it doesn't make her smile.

All day the train station has been filling with specials from New York City and the Pan-Am at Buffalo, travelers coming from every direction to see her fall. That's their music we can hear, the hurdy-gurdies playing from the pavilions and gazebos along the river.

"If it's my last night, I want to dance," she says to the dark and the river.

"It's not your last night," I tell her. Outside the lanterns circle, the world seems soft and still. I slowly pull her towards me. Although the song is faint, I recognize the tune, something about apple blossoms. We waltz on the deck in the dark, as well as I'm able. I've never been a dancer. Too soon I realize I've lost the rhythm of the song, I'm leading her to the thunder of the Falls.

"Cast me into the sea," she says again, her head against my shoulder, "so shall the sea become calm for you."

And maybe she believes it.

48 Sabotage – Davis

I have Burke dump man and mattress to the floor. From the way Russell hit the bottle last night, it hits him like a kick in the head.

"Where is she?" I ask. All he does is moan. He's still in his suit from last night. I have Burke frogmarch him down the stairs. "It's 30 to 1 she'll show!" I remind him. If she doesn't show, I can cover the spread, but I'll be damned if I won't take it from Russell's hide.

"Burke went to the boarding house looking for her, she never returned from the test run yesterday. After that damned cat died, she bolted. Coffee!" and the waiters come running. Russell takes the mug, wincing.

"Did she leave her luggage?" Russell asks.

"She never had any luggage! Just that damn barrel," and there's no sign of Ab. If he's gone to Forsyth for a better dollar, I'll see him flogged, I'll see him hanged.

"If she doesn't show, at least we won't go to jail for accessory to murder," Russell says, swallowing the coffee. He's gone so white he's green.

"No, I'll see you in jail for fraud. And who do you think is going to pay your bar tab? It was run against your winnings if she went over!" Ah, now that news has shook him awake.

"Wait a minute, I wasn't drinking alone, that was our investment in the press—to make sure we'd be on the front page." Listen to him spool, "It's our advertising, our—"

"—Your investment! Now find her or find fifty dollars," I tell him. Look at the fool, you can see his mind is working on escape, thinking he can sneak his bag from his room and make the train station without Burke's boot falling on his neck. He's wrong.

"I'll give you fifty to one she doesn't show," a mark says at my elbow.

"Book's closed! Burke, get him out of here!"

Burke doesn't even speak, just points his ginger beard at the mark and the man scatters.

"Dinan," Burke says and here the fool comes, two deputies flanking him.

"Where is she? The mad woman, where is she?" he shouts and I can see that Burke's got Russell by the collar to keep him from bolting.

"We don't know," I tell him. My mouth fills with bile. Telling truth to the law better not become a habit.

"Don't give me that rot! You've got a crowd near ten thousand on the wall of the Gorge waiting for her!" Well let Dinan shout and stamp, she's not here.

"And they're going to go on waiting, we don't know where she is," I say.

"Well when you find her, I've got a warrant and a doctor with a straight jacket and we're going to put her in Thornhill Asylum for her own protection," Dinan says, then gives a nod to his deputies and marches out.

"On whose dime?" I shout at his back. Dinan's arrival smells of wet dog and rotten egg. It smells of Forsyth. But then again, an asylum's not enough action for him. He usually sharpens the blade himself. Unless—I cross the lobby and pull the velvet drape off the barrel.

"Jesus!"

Barrel sitting on an anvil! No, barrel bolted to an anvil! Holes in the wood reeking of pitch!

"Burke!" I knew it—sabotage! An anvil—a goddamn noose around the neck! I will kill Forsyth for this, kill Russell, kill Ab—but I'll see my money first. "Get me that woman and get me a barrel, any barrel!" Thirty to one, I'll make that a sure thing if I have to wrestle her into the barrel myself.

"Mrs. Taylor," Burke says. And here's the charm, crisp and clean like a set of fresh sheets. And with her Ab, on guard.

"Thank God you're here, Mrs. Taylor," Russell says and stumbles over to her, "I've some bad news about your barrel." She crosses to the barrel and circles it with the look of a man trying to decide whether to buy a horse.

"It looks perfect, thank you," she says to Ab, like he's served her tea in a china cup. Always polite, the little twist.

"You ordered this—a hundred pound anvil?" Russell asks, loose jawed.

"Fifty pounds," she says, "I could explain the scientific theory behind it, but I'm sure you can think of a lie that will sell better than the truth."

"You're going to kill yourself with that!" Russell says. I nod at Burke and he moves his hand back to hold Russell's collar. He squeaks and goes silent. Let her kill herself, let her wrap herself in chain links if she wants, but let her fall.

"Isn't that what you're betting on?" she asks and looks at me, "That I'll go over and get killed."

She's right again. Russell placed a dollar on her falling, then bet another that she'd never walk away.

"I'm ready," she says, "Ab, please put the barrel in the wagon." Burke moves to help him. There's no walking the barrel, not with that anvil on it. With a dead lift they start out of the lobby.

"Just a moment," Russell says and pulls a letter from his jacket. "Addendum to our contract." She scans it.

"I'll sign it in front of the reporters," she says and Russell smiles at her.

"There's hope for you yet," he tells her.

I watch Ab and Burke load the barrel into the wagon. The air goes sulfur with camera flashes, all those shots of her with the anvil at her feet and the top of the barrel cresting her head. Damn it, they should have taken the shots in the lobby, in front of the goddamn fountain! She starts to read Russell's contract to the press.

"I have been influenced by no one. The idea to go over Niagara Falls was my own and I carried out all the preliminaries, including the design of the barrel, without assistance from anyone. If the trip is to mean my death, I fully and completely exonerate Frank M. Russell from any complicity in it," she finishes reading and signs the paper. The flashes explode as she hands the contract back to Russell.

"Any last words?" a reporter calls out.

"Yes. Mr. Davis?" she calls to me, "I have five dollars that says I will survive the Falls. What are the odds?"

"That you'll be crippled? Or that you'll walk away?" I call back.

"That I'll walk away," she says. God love the charm, not even a tremor at the question. So here's the answer.

"100 to 1!" I got her then. She can't help herself, she gasps. Then she smiles and holds the bill out to me. "It's a sure thing," she says and the reporters cheer.

I pocket her bill. I'm sure it's mine forever. But if she escapes, if she survives, I can find a way to make her survival pay.

49 The Rough – Annie

"Don't forget this," I say and hand Ab the bicycle pump. A crowd has gathered around the wagon. Ab holds a hand down for me. I put my boot in the spoke of the wheel and climb up. Then it's a slow turn—Russell swore it had to be slow—to face the crowd.

Lord, there's so many of them, a sea of faces in every direction. I force myself to smile at them. Half of them are willing me to quit, are even betting that I'll fail. But the others, the ones who believe in me, they need a last image of a happy woman. It will make it easier if I die, to see me now, fearless and fancy free. It will make it easier for Stilwell.

I see him working his way towards the wagon, elbowing his way through the crowd. His arms are filled with blue and white ticking, it's the coverlet from his bed, from last night, my last night.

I ache. To be open again after so long, it felt new. And the weight of Stilwell's body pressed against mine has left me lighter. I have always been seeking the smooth path, to limit sharps and angles. But to have the rough scrape of his calloused hands, the bristle of his cheek—I see now I should have spent more time looking for the rough that could make me smooth. Stilwell hands up the coverlet.

"Wrap this around you," he says. Ab takes the coverlet and places it in the bottom of the wagon. I want to jump down into Stilwell's arms. Instead, I wave at him, at the crowd, fearless and free.

Sealed – Ab

Ledge watches the water for Dinan and the deputies. I push the coverlet against the bottom of the barrel and along the sides. I take my knife and cut a hole in the fabric so that it fits 'round the cork in the breathing hole.

"You want a pillow for your head?" I ask Miss Annie. "Might be handy to have something between you and the lid."

"The barrel won't tip me over onto my head," she says. The pillow doesn't fit her calculations.

I cut two more slits in the coverlet and pull the leather straps through the ticking. The inside of the barrel smells of pitch and oak and leather. With the cotton batting that's pulled through the ticking it'll be as tight as swaddling.

"It's ready," I say. She's taken off her hat and put it in the bottom of the boat.

I tilt the barrel on its side and Miss Annie gets on her hands and knees. She starts to back into the barrel. She gets her boots in and stops.

"I can't do it," she says.

"I knew it!" Ledge shouts and starts jumping up and down. "She's not going over, Davis owes me a fiver!"

"Shut up or I'll toss you in the river!" I shout. Ledge stops, shrinks back a step. I crouch down next to Miss Annie.

"What's wrong?"

"With the coverlet and the harness, there's not enough room for me," she says. She doesn't lift her head, she's talking down to the mud.

"You need that padding, Miss Annie," I tell her.

"I won't fit," she says again, "I won't fit unless I take off my dress."

I hear Ledge pull his breath in sharp. I wait.

"Would you both please turn around?" she asks. I stand and nod at Ledge. We watch the trees. Dinan could be approaching but we can't watch the river for him. I start to hum, not to pass the time, but to know how much time is passing.

"It's all right. You can turn around now," she says.

I let Ledge turn around first.

"Damn it, I thought she wasn't going over," he says. I turn. Lying on her side in the barrel only her head is visible above the blue and white ticking of the coverlet.

"You have the harness on?" I ask. She nods.

"Please make sure that my dress doesn't get muddy," she says. She's folded it and placed it on the barrel lid. She plans to wear it again. I put it carefully in the bottom of the boat.

"Yes, Miss," I tell her. Ledge and I stand the barrel up. It won't balance on the anvil, and Ledge braces it upright.

"Have you bet any money, Ab?" she asks.

"Three months pay that you'll walk away," I tell her and she gasps.

"Three months!"

"Easy money, Miss."

She's quiet. There's just the sound of the river and the Falls. I wait.

"You can put the lid on now."

I take the lid and a mallet from the bottom of the boat. The lid is almost two inches thick. I slide it into place and tap it down. Then I lay the iron ring over the top of the barrel. Three months pay.

I seal her in.

51 Bound – Annie

I've been here before, in Ivan's shop. The wood comes down and blocks all light. There's a pause and a change in the pounding, from the mallet on the wood to the ring of metal on metal as the last ring is hammered into place.

It's done. I am bound in iron rings.

My knees already ache from crouching, they demand that I stand. I grab the cork and pull it out of the wall. A beam of light and a small current of air cut the darkness. I press my mouth to the hole.

"Are you ready to pump?" I ask Ab.

"Yes, Miss."

"Pump until you can't move the handle."

Ab threads the hose of the bicycle pump into the barrel and I close my hand around it, cutting off the light. As he begins to pump I feel the rush of air past my hand as the barrel fills with air. Stilwell taught me there are three falls, each one higher than the last. The padding is a bet that I'll need more cushion than air.

Ab jerks the hose out and I slip the cork back in. I bottle myself like a genii.

There are two taps on the lid of the barrel. I tap twice back to him. And then I begin to roll, sideways, onto my stomach, over to my back. There's a pause, and a muffled, "hoy!" and I'm in the boat. There's a pause, then a surge forward. We're pulling away from Cayuga Island, on the way to mid-stream, on the way to launch.

On my way to fall.

52 Foolkiller – Ab

We roll the barrel onto the rowboat. Ledge calls it the Foolkiller and maybe it is, maybe I'm the fool. Ledge mans the oars as I push us out into the current and climb in. The boat sits low in the water.

As soon as we clear the trees, the bettors can see us and the cheering starts.

"Look at them! Wait till Davis starts passing the basket—there's got to be 10,000 on the American side," Ledge says, pulling at the oars.

I keep my eyes on the water. I've never been this far downriver and the current is fast.

From around the point of Cayuga comes Dinan and the deputies.

"Pull to shore," Dinan yells. I can barely hear him over the sound of the crowd.

"Faster!" I yell at Ledge.

There's no helping it. The Sheriff's faster in the water. No barrel to weigh him down. He's gaining.

"Pull to shore!"

I hit the barrel twice. Miss Annie taps back. That's the signal.

I tip the barrel over and the boat rocks back as the weight leaves, it nearly swamps us.

I slide next to Ledge, take the left oar, and pull. We pull for our lives.

53 First – Annie

I hit the water on my side, then pop to standing as the anvil pulls down. I spin, round and round as I race for the edge. I tell myself it's a dance.

My boots are damp. The barrel must be leaking where the bolts hold the anvil. The pitch is too new, it hasn't fully dried. The coverlet must be wicking the water, soaking it up like a sponge as I spin, dancing towards the edge.

Four minutes from Cayuga Island I brace for the first fall.

54 The Book – Maude

Did you bet she wouldn't even get in the barrel? She'd turn chicken and wouldn't try? Well your good money's gone!

You can put down your binoculars, your wife's opera glasses, whatever you're spying with, 'cause there she is. There, floating low in the water. The thing that looks like a yellow hatbox skating towards the edge, that's her.

Shove the man next to you for a better view. Push him forward, against the railing. Push him towards the riverbank. Listen to the people scream.

"The pint glass! The pint glass!"

"The Queen of the Mist!"

"She's too close to the edge!"

"She'll fall to the side!"

"She'll smash on Table Rock!"

Tell them you've a five that says that she'll smash, 'cause the current is fast and the current is cruel.

"Easy money! Easy money!"

She's done for.

Second – Annie

I twist my neck, pull my face away from the coverlet. My eyes sting, slammed face down. Just the first. Fall.

Upright. My ears ring. I put my hands against the barrel lid. Push up. Hands to boots. Push up against the lid, push down with my feet. Make myself the center line. Brace myself for the second. Fall. Turn, turn quickly. Turn faster than my skirt can fall.

My hand hits the ground. Hard. The grass so dry it cuts. Cartwheel forward and David catches me. I can't breathe.

The crowd's so tight, too tight, pressing against us, no room for a reel but the fiddler keeps playing. David spins me, faster, faster, pressing me tighter and tighter against him.

There's water on my boots. The *pfeife* hitting the water, clinging to the barrel.

The barrel falls.

56 Deep – Maude

They'll say later that the barrel seemed to hang on the edge for a second, as if the wood itself were hesitating, pulling back.

They'll say it tipped forward slowly, as slow as a dancer bowing to his partner. From the Cave of the Winds they'll say they saw her, a glimmer of gold falling inside the green foam. Falling through the water, into water.

They'll say later that above the roar of the Falls you could hear Annie screaming. But no one will see her hit, see her crash. No one will see the anvil take her through the water curtain, down into the river's basin.

No one sees her fall deeper than the Falls are high.

No one sees her sink.

57 Bottom – Annie

There's a black spot on my mind. When I open my eyes I can't remember why it's so dark, so close, so cold.

Slam! Up and then forced down again. My teeth nearly crack. Bounce forward and then….stop.

Caught. The anvil's caught against something. What? A tree branch? A rock? No!

I bang against the barrel's wall. I lean forward and then back. Forward and back, pumping like a child on a swing. Throw myself against the walls, throw myself against the river. Inch forward, forward. I'm cold from the water.

The water's at my knees.

A screech. Me? Or metal against stone? My throat's raw. I'm screaming. Throw myself again and we slide forward, me and the barrel. An inch. And again, forward.

Free! Free as a pea from a shoot. The air in the barrel takes us up. Rise. Rise!

I stop rising and I start to spin. There's water at my waist. My hands cramp with cold. I can't watch. The baby's coffin is so tiny, as if I'm burying my boots.

But no, it's not the baby, it's David in the box, David sinking low into the ground. His big laugh laid down, locked beneath the wood and the dirt.

I strike the lid. My hand nearly breaks against the wood. I couldn't afford the oak casket, I had to take the pine. I bang on the lid. Hit it hard enough to hurt. The casket is filling with water. The barrel!

I find the cork and pull. Light!

I close my lips around the circle. I suck the air in and shake.

58 Cutoff – Stilwell

She breaks the surface! She's taken on water, she's taking on water, she's low. She's sinking!

Cheers from the Maid of the Mist as we four pull for her. Pull against the current. Pull against the wake.

Make the cut off.

Catch her before the river narrows.

Make the cutoff.

Cast the net.

Make the cut off.

Got her!

"Annie! Can you hear me?" I try to pull the net and barrel into the boat. It's no good, too heavy. The barrel's taken on too much water, if we try, it will swamp us. The best we can do is keep her close. Drag her in the net to shore. Pray that we're in time.

We reach the shallows by the launch. Burke jumps from the boat into the river. He steadies the barrel with his body.

"Hatchet!"

I drop the net. McIntire grabs it and I strike through the rope of the net. Smash the lid, cleave it in two and drop the pieces to the river.

Annie's eyes are closed, her lips blue. Water pools around her shoulders.

"Annie! Annie!" her eyes open, glassy. She's alive!

I grab her beneath her shoulders, but she's trapped by the harness.

"Knife, someone get me a knife!"

She closes her eyes and lets her head fall to the side. I pinch her ear till she cries out, her eyes open in panic. McIntire hands me a blade and I start to carve.

Wet feathers and leather come away in my hand, I toss them into the river. Finally I'm able to pull out one of her arms, then the other. I put them around my neck and tell her to hang on. She obeys, her head on my shoulder. Her skin is cold to the touch. Her breathing is ragged.

I pull her out. Cradle her. I wade back to the landing.

"Blankets! I need blankets!"

The tourists are coming down the gangplank towards us. They've their arms outstretched, already reaching for her, as if touching her will infect them with her courage.

Blankets! I wrap her in wool and pull her onto my lap. I will the heat to leave my body, to flow into her. Her teeth are chattering and blood courses down the left side of her face.

"A doctor! Where's the doctor?"

Burke dumps the barrel on its side, hoists it up on the landing next to us. He points at the crowd and a man with a black bag steps forward.

"You're the doctor?" I ask. He shakes his head.

"I'm the coroner."

"We don't need you!" I shout at him. If I could stand he'd be in the river now, he'd be facing the rapids, he'd be facing the whirlpool. Burke growls and the man disappears into the crowd.

"Make way for the press," here comes Russell with the ravens cawing behind him.

"You've just defeated the greatest waterfall in the world. What's your reaction?" a man asks, leaning in to her. She lifts her head from my shoulder, turns to face him.

"No one should ever do that again," she says. The pencils scribble. There's smoke from the flash. They've taken her picture, our picture.

"You couldn't think of anything better to say?" Russell hisses at her. "This is the national press!"

"I'm c-c-old," she says, "So c-cold."

"Get her to the hotel before she freezes to death," Russell tells Burke. And like that, the robber groom has her from my arms, has thrown me back into the shallows, is up the gangplank to the carriage.

"Watch the barrel!" Russell yells down to me.

Like that, she is saved and stolen away.

59 Recast – Russell

"No one should ever do that again?!" Christ! She sounded like a school m'arm. I should have had her memorize a line in advance, something like—"Fortune Favors the Brave!" or "So Dies the Undefeated Cataract!" Anything, anything other than "No one should ever do that again."

And the photo they took, wet and swaddled in the arms of that riverman. When they print it she'll look weak and helpless, she'll look old. Who'll pay to see that?

"You have to get her up!" I tell the doctor. "I've got press, national press, waiting for her! I've got a cake with candles, right in front of the Horseshoe fountain!" The doctor just squints at me. Hypothermia, concussion, I don't care what he calls it. Get her up for the photo! She only has to stand in the lobby! But no, she's to remain in bed, covered in hot water bottles.

"Let her just get up to make a wish and blow out the candles!" I tell him. "Five, ten minutes tops!" But he's resolute. He's Dinan's choice. If we could use Davis's doctor we'd be home free by now with the barrel, cake and Annie above the fold—but no, not if Dinan is involved.

I'll have to replace Annie Taylor. Keep the barrel, keep the story, but find some other woman. No, a girl. Yes, a little blonde. I can teach her. She can parrot Annie's story, answer the marks' questions. Smile for the photographs, fearless. Yes, right after the Pan-American I'll make my move and take the barrel with me.

Let Mrs. Taylor have her moment in Buffalo, but then I'm done with her. Let her chase me for the barrel if she wants, her story will sell better without her.

60 Roar – Stilwell

The nurse lets me in to see Annie because I saved her. Being the hero gets me bedside.

"She's going to be all right," she tells me in a quiet voice. Annie's arms lie straight atop the coverlet, the left wrist in a splint.

"She just needs rest and quiet," the nurse says.

I sit in the chair and stare at Annie. She was blue with cold and now she's a rising pink against the white of the sheets, pink as the rosebuds of the wallpaper. Her hair is plaited and lies over her right shoulder, like a girl's. Two nights ago I unwound that plait, shook out the pins from her hair. Now her head is wrapped around the forehead, a cut and a concussion for her troubles. She should be dead.

"You can hardly hear the Falls," the nurse says, "Mr. Davis has insulated the staterooms so well."

Still, Annie isn't peaceful. Her hands clench and unclench as she sleeps. There's a ragged spot in her breathing as if she's still trying to catch her breathe.

I want to ask her, what did it feel like to give into it? To let the water carry you forward, to have that moment of air before you fall?

What does it feel like to have the water hit you, to beat you down into the basin?

Is it over for her?

I know she felt it before, the pull of the Falls. I could see it in her eyes, the way she leaned forward, the way she reached for the edge. But does she feel it now? Is it ever over?

"No one should ever do that again," she told the press but I know that message was meant for me. Does that mean it didn't work, didn't cure her of the river's pull? Did it mean there's never any escape?

I shift in my chair. There's no creak of wood. There's only the hush.

The doctor enters. He frowns when he sees me. It's time to change the bandage on Annie's head and the nurse ushers me out. I stand outside her door and my boots sink into the carpet. There's a murmur, maybe it's the Falls beating back the muffling of the carpet and the horsehair insulating the walls. Maybe it's the murmur of the crowd still waiting for

Annie to come down the stairs, waiting for their Lazarus to arise.

I haven't moved. I swear I haven't moved from the chair in Annie's room, but here I am in the lobby, watching the water go over the Horseshoe fountain.

This miniature doesn't roar, it burbles. I swear at it under my breath. I will stay here and watch it. I will only leave this room to go back to Annie, to stay by her side.

But I'm outside, I'm standing in the mist. The rumble of the water comes up through the ground, up through my boots and into my bones.

My chest hurts. My heart was beating out of rhythm, my heart stopped, and now, with the roar of the Falls, it's restarted.

The Ring – Annie

I sleep for fourteen hours. Over my bed business continues. Mr. Davis counts out my winnings. Mr. Russell brings a hairdresser in to discuss the best hairstyle to hide the cut in my forehead. Then he brings her back an hour later to discuss how to emphasize it. Someone brings me a kitten, as white as Iagara. I can feel it climbing over the coverlet and even its slight weight makes me wince.

I try to wake, but every muscle screams for sleep. I think Stilwell watches over me. I think he is sitting by my bed, but when I force my eyes open I'm alone with the nurse. I sleep.

Hard white light and the drumming of hammers against my forehead. The doctor changes my bandage. He checks my eyes, my pulse, my breathing. I am well enough to get up, I tell him, and force a smile. I must make the Pan-American Exposition by tomorrow. I must start to tell my story or the fall will be for nothing.

The nurse helps me to dress. She tells me a friend is waiting. Before I can blush, I hear the laugh. Lydia!

It can't be, but here she is, sailing into the room in her passing outfit, a high collar and long gloves covering up her ink.

"Lydia!" I grab her tightly and nearly cry out as pain shoots up my arms.

"Miss Annie? You all right?" she asks, her large brown eyes are worried.

"Just bumps and bruises, nothing more," the nurse says and leaves us alone.

"After a fall like that, you must be black and blue all over," she laughs again, "Your skin might be more blue than mine."

"It's so good to see you. Are you on your way to the Pan-American?" I ask.

"I'm here on my honeymoon," she nearly chortles and strips off her glove with a flourish. A thin gold band circles a finger inked with twisting vines. "Would you like to meet him?" she doesn't wait for my answer, just flings the door open. "She's awake!" she calls and the broad form of Ivan Rozenski fills the doorway.

"Good Lord, Ivan!" I gasp.

"I'm glad to see the fall hasn't affected your memory," he says, stepping into the room. "There's 30,000 people a day at the Pan-American Exposition who need to hear you say my name."

"Ivan Rozenski, the only man who could build the only barrel that could survive," I say and my voice nearly breaks. "Congratulations," I manage.

"We have you to thank. You and your barrel," Lydia says as Ivan takes her hand.

"I've always had a soft spot for participatory women," Ivan says with a wink.

"We have a present for you," Lydia says and claps her hands with excitement.

Ivan pulls a small box from his jacket pocket and puts it in my hands. When I don't move to open it he waggles his finger at me.

"Have no fear, woman, it's not another hatchet."

"You heard about that?"

"Saginaw has newspapers," he replies and steps back. I'm stunned. Russell was right, my interview with Carrie Nation made the national press.

I open the box. It's my ring, my wedding ring from David. My eyes fill with tears.

"*Verdammit noch mal!*" Ivan stomps, "if you drop a single tear I'm taking it back to the pawn broker!"

"I had a dream—"

"—Well you're awake now," Ivan says. "The adventure's over, now the work begins."

"Are you ready?" Lydia asks.

I think of the spectators on the gangway, reaching for me as if they would tear at my clothes. I think of the newspapermen's questions and the choking smoke of the camera. I think of Russell's hot breath and his many, many lies.

I'm ready for anything

The Force – Dinan

When I arrive at the Table Rock Hotel with the deputies the doctor tells me Mrs. Taylor is too ill to stand. She's not well enough to arrest for attempted suicide. But I'm done with Davis's tricks. I'm sure he thinks he'll sneak her out the back door. Knowing him, he probably thinks he can parade her down the front stairs with the press and the people watching and I won't arrest her. He can think again.

I send the deputies to guard the doors and sit myself down in the bar to wait for her. From here I can see the stairs. I'm a patient man and the drinks are free.

It's two when they close the bar, right on time, that being the law. I sit myself in the lobby by the fountain. What need have I to go home? Even in the wee hours, my missus can still rouse herself to a fit about the widow woman and the little dead cat.

I put my head back. Davis calls these "wing chairs," these tall backs you can rest your head on. I dream of my wife. She's babbling as happily as the fountain.

"Johnny, I'm talking to you!" the missus shouts and I'm thrown awake. "Mrs. Taylor was just explaining how bicycles work. Johnny, you'll have to buy me one."

Good Lord, she's here! Standing in front of me in her Sunday meeting clothes. And beside her, pale but smiling, is the widow woman.

"You were soooo good, Johnny, to arrange this private interview with Mrs. Taylor," my missus says and the widow puts a hand on her arm.

"Please, call me Annie," the widow says and I can feel the heat rising up my collar.

"Did you now that it's very hard to fall off a bicycle once it's moving because there's a spinning force and the spinning force is bigger than the falling force and—how did you put it Annie, dear?" the missus says.

"Once the bicycle's wheels are spinning, their centrifugal force is greater than gravity," the widow says.

I don't know what the hell that means, but I can decipher Davis's smile as he walks into the room. My wife has made a friend and that friend gets to stay out of jail.

"Time we've gone home, Marie," I say as I stand.

"It's science, Johnny!" my missus says, "and now that I know the science I want to ride a bicycle."

I don't mark the rest as she needles it. There's no more sense to putting a woman on a bicycle than there is in giving her wings.

I give myself a week before she's got me flying over handlebars.

The Tip – Porter

Lord, how I hate the departure platform. It's a purgatory, with no money to be made. Travelers leave upended, penniless, little thought to the tip they'll need for the porter.

And few have need of us. They arrive with brides that can't be trusted to walk unaided across the platform, they leave with wives that can carry their own bags. They've learned their women might bruise, but they don't break.

And there's no color on this side, no one screaming at you to see this cliff or that cave. Just the postcard seller, leering at the travelers over his wooden tray. He's got photos of all the sites the travelers have seen, or should have seen, if they could rouse themselves from bed and find their pants.

He's the only one with hope for a wage. If they spent their week abed they'll buy the postcard seller out of what they'll later tell everyone they saw, when really they spent their days indoors roiling the sheets.

A carriage arrives but all hope of a tip dies when I see what it's transporting, the mad woman and her barrel.

For a vessel that's taken a beating, it gleams of varnish and it's lettered in gold "Queen of the Mist." And the widow, she's been frippered. I'd not have recognized her without the barrel and Davis's big Black.

There's a trill and the bicycle boy passes. I reach for my wallet. He moves through the crowd, circles the widow, and is given the shove off. She's taken to first class. The boy makes for arrivals, as would I, there's no money to be made here.

Wait. Here's a pair, all a flutter.

"Why not hand over that bag and take the missus's hand instead?" I say to him, and he does. Good lad.

"Postcards for sale! Get your postcards!"

It'll be a comedy, how many these two buy. They lean in, on common agreement, and then she startles.

"Good Lord, Malcolm, it's Miss Annie," she says, like she knows the character. I look over his shoulder at the postcard and there's the madwoman staring back at me, her hand on that cursed egg of a barrel. I look away.

There's danger in those photos. You'd think this woman went over and that's the end of the Falls, conquered and closed up. But there's something in her eyes that says "follow me."

Mark my words, she won't be the last to lock herself up and go over. There's those that will look too long and too hard at those photos. They'll stare till they start thinking they, too, need a race over the edge of the world.

64 Marvels – Annie

When I look through the flap in the tent all I can see are nymphae floating on the surface of the water. The fountain's basin is filled with their lily pads.

Russell has planted us on the promenade between the Hall of Music and the Tower of Electricity. I can hear its fountain gushing, a recreation of the Bridal Veil Falls. It has a vicious reach, shooting out ten feet from the tower's second story before falling. It's an advertisement for the source of the park's energy, the hydro-electricity coursing the 25 miles from Niagara Falls.

I clench and unclench my hands in the bucket. All that soothes them is a cold water soak. Two shows a day and your ticket price comes with the privilege of shaking my hand. We've two days to go before the close and soon I will not be able to get on my gloves. Still, with the gate Russell's collecting, I can buy myself a hundred pair.

If I'm veiled, I can walk through the park and tour the exhibits without drawing attention. Russell's stressed that no one is to meet me who hasn't paid for the privilege.

It's hard to believe the buildings are just plaster. They look as solid as marble, with wide steps and Doric columns. The best of Paris, Vienna and Rome has been recreated here, with wide boulevards and lush gardens. Statues dot the landscape, an Apollo five times the size of a man drives his chariot across the sky, the Children of Lir, caught in the moment they change into swans, raise their wings. And everything is studded with light bulbs, thousands of them blazing. At night the park glitters as if it were set by Tiffany. But come December, they'll all be plowed into the ground.

I've seen mechanical marvels, and yesterday, I saw my first miracle, a device that harnesses invisible rays, X-rays, to show us the unseen. A man standing between the X-ray device and a metal plate left behind the image of his own skeleton. It was as if we could see his death as it waited quietly inside him.

Soon they will harness it to show us the invisible liquid of the soul, and even our own thoughts. Perhaps then we will know our own minds, when they develop before us and we can page through them like a book.

I dry my hands and fish the salve from my new reticule, it's a new purchase, my first in five years. I'm told it's called a purse. Its clasp makes the satisfying click of heavy coins dropping one atop another. I work the salve into the swollen places around my knuckles.

I've an invitation to appear in Ziegfeld's Follies. Russell fixed it so that I emerge from a trick barrel, the staves falling away from me in a puff of smoke. But New York audiences tire quickly; if I'm to stretch the week's guarantee Russell tells me I need an act—a song, a dance, a series of jokes. "Snappy patter," Russell calls it. How many jokes are there about falling for your life?

I put the salve away and pull out the packet of newspaper clippings about my fall. Each one gets the story wrong. *The New York Times* calls me "Minnie Taylor," *The New York World* claims I'm 63! Still the stories lay the ground for our travels, New York, Philadelphia, Baltimore, D.C. and then west to Pittsburgh, Cleveland and Chicago.

I don't know how long my story will sell. I measure each day's take in warm rooms and hot meals. How far can my freedom stretch? Already there's talk of a man going over the Falls, an act that will eclipse me. So many of the men that come to my show and stay to shake my hand, I can feel them sizing me up and deciding that if I could survive the fall, then anyone could.

Russell doesn't mind them, he encourages them. For an extra dollar they can climb inside the barrel to try it out.

"Fools going to slaughter," he calls them. He tells me more disasters at the Falls will increase my fame. But no one should ever do it again.

The day we arrived in Buffalo I found half a postcard in my bag. It was me with the barrel in front of Saul Davis's fountain, except the picture of me had been torn away and only the barrel was left. On the back is printed, "I cannot leave. I will not follow."

Stilwell must have paid the bicycle boy to slip it into my bag that day on the departure platform. He must have kept the half of the postcard with my picture. Somewhere I am staring back at him.

"I cannot leave," I understand. He is chained to the Falls. They are his oxygen and without them he will smother. But "I will not follow," for days I was angry at those words, as if I had asked him to be my escort, carry my bags, warm my bed. But now I think he means he won't let the Falls pull him in, won't give into the push of the current, won't follow me over the Falls. "I will not follow" means he is not free, but he is safe. It will have to be enough.

"Five minutes to curtain!" Russell calls and already I can hear the crowd murmuring. Russell warms them up with the facts about the Falls, their height, their breadth.

"Blink!" he tells them, "and a million gallons fall. Blink again! Another million!"

Next is danger and disaster. He calls this section, "They Tried and Died!" The more gruesome the demise, the better.

He seems to delight in the shattered wood, the bloated bodies, the severed arms.

"Ladies and Gentlemen! She thought the Unthinkable! She Broke the UnBreakable! She Braved the UnFathomable! She's the Dowager of Daredevils! The Darling of Disaster! The Queen of the Cataract!"

The curtain parts, and my wide smile is met with confusion. The audience shifts in their seats, still applauding as they try to see past me to the woman Russell has described.

"Ladies and Gentlemen!

The Inimitable, Formidable, and Absolutely Unsinkable —Annie Edson Taylor!"

I place one hand on the barrel that should have been my coffin and slowly sweep my other arm in a wide arc that takes in the crowd, the fair, the future, and everything after it.

ACKNOWLEDGEMENTS

Many thanks to: Marie Cantin and Michael Miner, who encouraged me to pursue Annie's story; Kate O'Connell, my editor extraordinaire; Brad Griffith, for his many voices; Diane Machado for her elegant design; the friendly readers who encouraged earlier drafts; the coopers at Old Sturbridge Village, who patiently answered my barrel questions; and the librarians and archivists who assisted me in compiling information about the daredevils of Niagara and their stunts.

Last and best, my heartfelt thanks to Roger, who carved out the time.

ABOUT THE AUTHOR

Photo: John Rybicki

Katerie Morin is a playwright whose work
has been produced in the U.S., published
in China, and broadcast in New Zealand.
She received her M.F.A in Playwriting from the
University of Washington and her B.A. from
Smith College. She lives outside of Boston
with her family.

Made in the USA
Monee, IL
14 April 2020

25760249R10157